‹] **W9-APR-204**

*Dear Diary,*

*The Matchmaking Mamas have found our latest project! There are lots of lonely hearts to heal this Christmas, but we've discovered a special twosome that we hope will meet under the mistletoe on December 25.*

*Keith O'Connell is a handsome lawyer who's headed home for the holidays...but not to celebrate with his family. Sadly, he was estranged from his mother, who's since passed away. Now he's back in town to sell his childhood home.*

*So far, we have seen a few signs of Keith opening up to someone, a woman he's known for years. She's beautiful and smart, and she seems to be luring him out of his shell, bit by bit, this holiday season.*

*I know Kenzie Bradshaw had a crush on Keith back in junior high, but they're both all grown up now. And she's still got a thing for the guy in a buttoned-up suit with a closed-off heart. Keith is one puzzle that Kenzie is determined to unravel, but will they realize how perfect they are together in time for Christmas? I can't wait to watch and find out.*

*Love,*

*Maizie*

*Matchmaking Mama Extraordinaire*

Dear Reader,

Sometimes, it takes me a while to come up with a story. On other occasions, the story just leaps up at me. And then there are the stories that come in waves. This is one of those.

My German shepherd, Audrey Hepburn (the rescue society named her), was very skittish when she came into our home. Initially, she was afraid of everything, including other dogs, so I would walk her at 5:30 every morning. But there was this one house with a superfriendly black Labrador, Pi, in the yard. Pi would come running out when he saw her and Audie would hide behind me.

To get her over this, I took to carrying dog treats with me. I'd hold one out to Pi and another to Audie. Ever so slowly, I'd bring the treats in closer and I got her to edge forward to the fence. Success came when they got so close, their noses touched—and Audie didn't flee. This became our daily routine.

Every time we passed Pi's yard, Audie would look to see if he was there. Then, just like that, Pi wasn't there anymore. Several weeks later, there was an outdoor awning in front of Pi's house with an Estate Sale sign. I was told that Pi's "mother" had passed away and her family was selling the house. Pi ended up living with the woman's daughter.

As always, I thank you for taking the time to read my book, and from the bottom of my heart, I wish you someone to love who loves you back.

Love,

Marie Ferrarella

# Coming Home
# for Christmas

—

## Marie Ferrarella

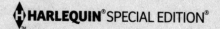
HARLEQUIN® SPECIAL EDITION®

If you purchased this book without a cover you should be aware that this book is stolen property. It was reported as "unsold and destroyed" to the publisher, and neither the author nor the publisher has received any payment for this "stripped book."

Recycling programs
for this product may
not exist in your area.

ISBN-13: 978-0-373-65919-7

Coming Home for Christmas

Copyright © 2015 by Marie Rydzynski-Ferrarella

All rights reserved. Except for use in any review, the reproduction or utilization of this work in whole or in part in any form by any electronic, mechanical or other means, now known or hereinafter invented, including xerography, photocopying and recording, or in any information storage or retrieval system, is forbidden without the written permission of the publisher, Harlequin Enterprises Limited, 225 Duncan Mill Road, Don Mills, Ontario M3B 3K9, Canada.

This is a work of fiction. Names, characters, places and incidents are either the product of the author's imagination or are used fictitiously, and any resemblance to actual persons, living or dead, business establishments, events or locales is entirely coincidental.

This edition published by arrangement with Harlequin Books S.A.

For questions and comments about the quality of this book, please contact us at CustomerService@Harlequin.com.

® and TM are trademarks of Harlequin Enterprises Limited or its corporate affiliates. Trademarks indicated with ® are registered in the United States Patent and Trademark Office, the Canadian Intellectual Property Office and in other countries.

**Printed in U.S.A.**

www.Harlequin.com

*USA TODAY* bestselling and RITA® Award-winning author **Marie Ferrarella** has written more than two hundred and fifty books for Harlequin, some under the name Marie Nicole. Her romances are beloved by fans worldwide. Visit her website, marieferrarella.com.

To
Elliana Melgar,
Welcome
To
The
World

## *Prologue*

It felt very odd to be back.

In all honesty, he never thought he'd be back here again. Not back in this city. Certainly not back in this house.

But then, he never thought his mother would become someone he'd be forced to think of in the past tense, either.

Granted, he and his mother hadn't spoken in almost ten years. But despite his criticism the last time words—angry, hot words—had been exchanged between them, she had always struck him as being a force of nature. Forces of nature didn't just cease to exist. They continued. Whether or not someone was there to witness the force, it continued.

Somewhere in his unconscious, he had thought his mother would be the same way. She would just continue.

But Dorothy O'Connell didn't continue. Quite abruptly, without any warning, without any lingering diseases, her heart just suddenly gave out and she died. If it hadn't been for the phone call he'd received from her neighbor, he wouldn't even have known this had transpired.

Well, now he knew. Knew when there was nothing further he could do about it. Knew that there would never be an opportunity to mend the rift that had existed between them.

Not that there would have been much chance of that, even if she were still alive and they had another twenty years. The wounds had gone too deep.

And he had lost his mother long before he'd walked out of the house that day.

Keith sighed as he looked around the first-floor family room. You would think, after ten years—and knowing that she was gone—he wouldn't expect to see her come walking into the room. Wouldn't, on some level, strain to hear the sound of her voice as she called out to him, or to Amy.

Or both.

The house had always been filled with her voice and her presence. At least, he amended, for most of the years he'd lived in it. It was only after—after the car accident—after Amy wasn't around anymore—that everything changed.

And somehow, in an odd sort of way, it had stayed the same. Except tenser. So much tenser. He supposed that part of it had been his fault, too.

Keith shrugged even though there was no one there to see him do so. No one there to call him on it.

It didn't matter. All the tension, the things that were said, the things that *weren't* said, none of it mattered anymore. It was all in the past now.

Just like his mother was in the past.

He was here. Here to tie up all the loose ends, to tend

to the arrangements. To shut down that chapter of his life and put it all away in a box.

After all, life went on. Except, of course, when it didn't.

Keith resisted the fleeting temptation to go upstairs and look into rooms he hadn't looked into in ten years. There was no point to that. He wasn't here to thumb a ride down memory lane. He was here for one purpose only: to sell the house and everything in it. The items in the house were of no use to him and hadn't been for a very long time.

Squaring his shoulders, Keith got down to business. The sooner he was finished, the sooner he could get back to the firm up north in San Francisco and to his life.

And forget all about the house on Normandie in Bedford and the woman who had lived in it.

## Chapter One

With her trim figure and attractively styled light blond hair, Maizie Sommers looked far younger than the actual years noted on her birth certificate. She liked to tell people that her family and her real estate company kept her vital and young, which was true.

And then there was her other hobby, the one she was involved in with Theresa and Cecilia, her two best friends since the third grade. The hobby that, she firmly believed, aided her in finally getting the son-in-law and grandchildren she'd always hoped for. She, Theresa and Cecilia were very skilled at, quite unashamedly, matchmaking.

Specifically, covert matchmaking. The unassuming objects of their selfless efforts were never aware of what hit them when love came barreling into their lives.

The matchmaking tasks were usually undertaken at the behest of either one unwitting participant's relative or the other, most often a parent. And the ladies happily took it from there.

As it turned out, they were enabled in their altruistic endeavors because of the companies they had formed during the second half of their lives. After each woman had raised her child—or, in Theresa's case, children—and found herself squarely faced with widowhood, all three friends had met the resulting emptiness in their lives the same way. They turned their attention to whatever skills they had and transformed those into what eventually amounted to lucrative livelihoods. Maizie went into real estate, Theresa undertook catering and Cecilia, always the very last word in organization and neatness, began her own housecleaning service.

Each of these three businesses, now quite nicely successful, brought into their collective lives an ever-changing and growing pool of people.

It was within this pool that the three friends found their likely candidates: unattached people who were in need of soul mates in order to reach their own full potential and thrive.

Maizie, Theresa and Cecilia thought of their matchmaking as a calling.

Even as they conducted business as usual, all three women were on the lookout for their next matchmaking success stories.

And none was as proactive as Maizie, whose cache of candidates was always changing.

Maizie had an eye not just for excellent property buys, which in turn were responsible for bringing money into her company, but also for loneliness, no matter how well disguised that loneliness might be within the person who crossed her path.

Such was the case, she felt, with her latest client. The tall, good-looking young man walked into her office on a Wednesday morning, wearing a somber expression and an expensive gray suit. He had green eyes and very precisely cut thick, dark brown hair, and his incredible straight-arrow posture made his broad shoulders appear even broader than they were.

"Maizie Sommers?" Keith asked as he approached her desk.

He'd gotten her name from the same neighbor who had notified him of his mother's sudden passing. He felt one real estate firm was as good as another, but perhaps a smaller one was a little hungrier than a corporation so the agent could be persuaded to sell the house faster. At least, that was his reasoning when he'd found her on the internet and then came here immediately after that.

Maizie looked up into his eyes and gave the young man her best maternal smile. It usually went a long way in disarming her prospective clients and getting them to trust her.

She didn't do it for any devious or self-serving purpose. What she was trying to convey to her clients was that it wasn't a matter of her versus them but a matter of them *and* her. She thought of herself and her clients as a team, and she intended to be on her clients' side.

Sales were not final until the clients were happy with the home they were buying. She took any misgivings they might entertain very seriously. Their ultimate satisfaction was *always* her bottom line.

And if, along the way, said client also turned out to be an unattached person who would be decidedly happier as part of a twosome—Maizie was a very firm believer in love—well, so much the better.

That part of what she and her friends did—the matchmaking—was undertaken without any thought— or collection—of financial rewards. Maizie, Theresa and Cecilia all unequivocally believed that the soul needed nurturing as well as the body. And in the case of their matchmaking efforts, with each success—and thus far, they had *only* successes—they felt even more fulfilled than they did when the actual.jobs they did collect fees for were successfully executed.

Thus, until she knew otherwise, Maizie viewed the young man who walked into her office this morning as quite possibly a candidate on two fronts.

The smile on her lips came from deep within.

"Yes, I am, young man," she told him warmly. "What can I do for you?" she asked, rising ever so slightly from the seat behind her desk to shake his hand.

The woman reminded him of his mother.

It wasn't so much that this Maizie Sommers he had come to see actually resembled his mother visually, but there was an enthusiasm—as well as a kindness—that seemed somehow to *radiate* from this woman. Such was often the case with his mother.

At least, his mother the way she had been those years when he was growing up. The years before Amy had died. The three of them had been a happy unit then, bolstering one another. And no matter what, he and Amy had always been secure in the knowledge that although there was no father in the picture for a good deal of the time, all was well in their lives because their mother was with them. They were convinced Dorothy O'Connell could handle anything. Nothing would ever hurt them as long as she was around.

It turned out to be a lie.

Keith realized that he had lapsed into silence when he should be saying *something*. Attempting to recover ground, Keith cleared his throat and took a stab at apologizing, something he hardly ever did.

"Sorry, I didn't mean to stare," he said, deliberately

averting his eyes from her. "For a minute, you reminded me of someone."

Maizie's bright blue eyes crinkled at the corners as she smiled at him. "A pleasant memory, I hope."

"Yes, well, it was. Once," he allowed, stumbling ever so slightly over the words coming out as he continued looking away.

"I see," she responded, hoping he'd continue. Her prospective client appeared to be somewhat uncomfortable, though. One of the things she prided herself on the most, an ability she had honed both as a mother and as a successful independent businesswoman, was putting someone at ease.

Glossing over the young man's last words, Maizie purposely went on to the reason she assumed that he had come to her in the first place. In her judgment, he appeared to be the type who was more comfortable sticking to the business at hand than touching upon anything even remotely personal.

Still, she couldn't help wondering if he was married or, at the very least, spoken for. The young man was clearly the kind who fell into the "drop-dead gorgeous" category, as Cecilia's daughter liked to say. If he wasn't married, well then, she just might have met her newest challenge.

"Are you here looking to buy a house, Mr...." She let her voice trail off, giving him the opportunity to state exactly why he was here as well as introduce himself.

"Oh, sorry." Keith upbraided himself. He really wasn't on his game today. Going straight from the airport to the house and then staying there overnight had done that to him. He would have been better off booking a hotel room.

He was going to have to see to that as soon as he finished up with this woman.

"Keith O'Connell," he told her, shaking her hand be-

latedly. Given their proximity and difference in height—
Maizie was petite while he was six-foot-two—he didn't
have to lean over her desk because she was standing up.
"And I'm looking to sell, not buy, actually."

"Sell," she repeated slowly, as if she was pausing to
taste the word. "You own a home here in Bedford?" she
asked.

"In a manner of speaking."

He couldn't think of himself as being the actual owner.
That had been his mother, who had worked long and hard,
stitching together disjointed hours so she could be home
for Amy and him when they were younger and needed
her, but still provide for them. It was his mother's sweat
and dedication that had managed to pay for the house.
He had just lived there—until he didn't. And now it was
his by default.

Because there was no one left.

"It is—*was*," Keith corrected himself, "my mother's
house."

Maizie sensed another wave of discomfort sweeping
over her client-to-be and interpreted it the only way she
could. He was having second thoughts about the fate of
the house.

"Are you sure you want to sell it?" she questioned
gently.

"Yes." The single word was emphatic, exploding from
his lips almost like a gunshot. And then Keith backped-
aled just a shade. "I live and work in San Francisco, and
there's no reason for me to maintain a house down here.
I'd like to sell the house as quickly as possible," he added.

Maizie had remained on her feet. "Well, then, let's go
take a look at it, shall we?" she suggested brightly.

Keith nodded. "My car's parked in front of the restaurant," he told her. Striding ahead of the agent, he opened the office's front door and held it for her.

Maizie glanced over her shoulder at the young woman seated at a desk in the corner. "I should only be gone for a little while, Rhonda. Hold down the fort," she instructed her assistant cheerfully.

The woman she addressed looked as if she was eager to be the only occupant of the "fort."

"Yes, ma'am!"

"She's in training," Maizie confided to her client-to-be once they were outside the office and the door had closed behind them. "More willing than able at the moment, I'm afraid. But with luck that should change soon." At least, she hoped so. "We'll take my car," she announced as she stopped in front of a cream-colored Mercedes.

Keith glanced over toward his own dark blue sedan parked several yards away. He was accustomed to taking charge, no matter what the situation. He was also accustomed to being the one behind the wheel. "I thought that—"

Maizie neatly cut him off, her maternal smile widening considerably.

"No reason for you to use up your gas," she informed him cheerfully. Aiming her key fob at her vehicle, she pressed it, and a melodious signal announced that the door locks had been released.

Without hesitation, Maizie got in, buckled up, then looked to her right and waited. After a beat, her would-be client got in on the passenger's side. She hadn't quite comprehended how tall the man was until he more than filled that section of her vehicle.

Hands resting on the steering wheel, she paused until Keith buckled up before saying, "Now, if you just give me the address, we'll be on our way."

Keith gave her the house number, adding, "That's in the—"

"West Park development," Maizie acknowledged. She flashed a smile at Keith as she pulled away from the curb. "I've been at this for a while now," she told him.

*Good for you*, Keith thought as he stared, sphinxlike, straight ahead through the front windshield. With luck, this would wind up being one of his last drives to his mother's house.

"It's a lovely home," Maizie concluded after her tour of both floors, the three-car garage and the backyard.

She preferred to build up her own rapport with the house she was to sell, but many of her clients insisted on leading the tour. She'd noticed Keith had hung back a little after he'd unlocked the front door.

It was very evident he had no desire to be here.

Either that or Keith was reluctant about selling the house in the first place but found himself in a financial situation forcing him to take this path.

"How fast can you sell it?" he asked her abruptly the moment he saw that she had finished her initial inspection.

Maizie watched her newest client for a long moment, studying him before she finally replied.

"I'm afraid that all depends on the market, the price of the house, what you—"

"You do it," he said abruptly.

"Do what, exactly?" Maizie asked. He looked to be on edge. Why? she wondered. Did it have to do with the house or something else? There were a lot of gaps she would have to fill. It didn't necessarily help with the sale of the house, but the information would be useful in other ways.

"You determine the going price for the house and sell it for just under that," he explained.

"Under the going rate?" Maizie questioned. Why would he want to sell it short? This was one of the more popular models in the development, and its orientation was ideal. The morning sun hit the kitchen and family room first. By the time the afternoon arrived with its heat, the sun was hitting the driveway, leaving the house enveloped in comfort.

Maizie looked at her new client more closely. "What's wrong with the house, Mr. O'Connell?"

"Nothing." He had to hold himself in check to keep from snapping. That wasn't going to help. Besides, it wasn't Mrs. Sommers's fault that closure felt as if it was eluding him. "There's nothing wrong with the house. I just want to get rid of it. I told you, I don't live in this area anymore, and I just want to sell the house and get back to my work."

"What is it that you do, Mr. O'Connell?"

"I'm a lawyer." Usually he experienced a tinge of pride accompanying that sentence. But this time there was nothing, just this odd, hollow feeling, as if being a lawyer didn't matter anymore.

That was ridiculous. Of course it mattered. He was just fatigued, Keith insisted, silently scolding himself for the irrational thought.

"A lawyer," Maizie repeated with an approving nod of her head, surprising him. "The son and daughter of one of my best friends are both lawyers," she told him conversationally. And then she sobered slightly and she asked in as kind a tone as she could, "Did your mother die at home, by any chance?"

Because if the woman had, that put an impedance on the idea of a quick sale. Legally, at-home deaths had to be stated as such, and there were a great many people who wouldn't dream of buying a home that supposedly came with its very own ghost to haunt its hallways.

Keith blinked. "What? No. Why?" The single-word sentences were fired out at her like bullets, shot one at a time.

Maizie's tone continued to be kind as she answered him. "I thought that might explain why you seem so… tense," she finally said for lack of a better word.

She didn't want to offend the young man, but she did want to get to the heart of what might be troubling him, because he *was* troubled. Anyone could see that.

"Jet lag," Keith told her dismissively, as if that explained everything.

"San Francisco is in the same time zone," she pointed out gently. There was no reason for him to be experiencing any sort of jet lag.

"Of course it's in the same time zone. I'm not an idiot," Keith protested. "Sorry," he murmured, doing his best to bank down his temper. Over the years, he'd schooled himself to be emotionally reserved. But what he'd learned was escaping him right now. "I was in New York on business when I got the call that—" Abruptly he changed the course of his response, correcting his last words. "My firm took a call from my mother's neighbor saying that my mother had passed away. My assistant called me. So I caught the next plane back," he told her.

And then he stopped cold.

Keith wasn't accustomed to explaining himself. He hadn't done that in a very long time. This had all caught him completely by surprise, and he was revealing more than he'd intended.

"That doesn't have anything to do with anything," he informed her stiffly.

"No," she agreed, "it doesn't. But I was just trying to get a feeling for the situation—and you. It helps me do a better job." Maizie knew she had to sell this to the young man, who needed far more than the sale of this house to tie up loose ends.

He needed peace, she thought.

"I don't care what you get for it. Just sell it," Keith was saying. "I don't want it hanging around my neck like the proverbial albatross."

"You might not care about the sale price now, but you will someday soon. Perhaps even very soon." Maizie paused, her sharp eyes sweeping over everything in the living room. "If you don't mind my asking, what are you planning on doing with the furnishings?"

"Furnishings?" Keith repeated uncomprehendingly.

"The furniture, the clothing in the closets, the books—"

He hadn't even thought about that. He supposed he was still coming to grips with the idea that as far as his mother was concerned, there would be no more tomorrows and all that entailed.

Replaying the agent's words in his head, Keith waved his hand, dismissing the problem. "Get rid of it. All of it." The things she'd enumerated represented a place in his life he had no intention of revisiting. "Throw it all away."

That would be a terrible waste, and Maizie wasn't about to be wasteful if she could possibly help it. "I think if you do that, if you just throw all this away, you'll live to regret it."

He was already regretting this conversation. However, he told himself that it cost him nothing to hear her out. "All right. What do you suggest?"

Maizie thought of the conversation she'd just had yesterday with Theresa over a late lunch. It involved the daughter of a mutual friend.

The *single* daughter of a mutual friend.

A wide smile blossomed on Maizie's lips. "I think I have an idea you just might like."

## Chapter Two

"You do realize you work too hard, right?"

Marcy Crawford aimed the question at her younger sister, MacKenzie Bradshaw, as she followed her sister around a showroom that was nothing short of an obstacle course for anyone who wasn't a size three. And in her current state of pregnancy, Marcy admittedly hadn't been a petite size three for a little longer than eight months now.

Her question was a rhetorical one, and it was meant to get Kenzie, the youngest of five and the one everyone in the family doted on, to reassess her present life. However, her supposedly impromptu visit to Kenzie's place of work wound up getting the latter to fall back on her usual evasive maneuvers. Whether or not she actually meant to, Kenzie was weaving her way in and out of small pockets of space. Pockets that Marcy was frustratingly finding close to impossible to get into. Thus she was completely unable to follow.

Kenzie glanced over her shoulder, pausing only long

enough to blow her light blond bangs out of her eyes—she *had* to find time to get a haircut, she silently noted. With Christmas almost here, business had been good lately, really good. The turnaround at her shop, Hidden Treasures, both with items coming in and going out, had been more than a little gratifying.

"Said the woman who's more than eight months pregnant and carrying a fourteenth-month-old around in her arms," Kenzie pointed out.

She dearly loved her sister—loved all four of her siblings and her mother—but she instantly went into withdrawal mode the moment Marcy or the others felt compelled to change around the structure of her life. She liked it just the way it was—busy and profitable.

"Exactly my point," Marcy said, shuffling so that she was finally able to move in front of her sister by coming in from the other side. The less than fluid movement managed to trap Kenzie with an ornate carved turn-of-the-century credenza at her back while she, with her sheer girth, barred her sister's escape from the front. "All this effort you keep putting out, it should be going toward your own family, not toward pawing through dead people's junk."

"Hidden treasures," Kenzie corrected her with just a touch of indignation, taking offense for both her clients and the one-of-a-kind items in her shop. "One woman's junk is another woman's prized possession."

"Call it whatever you like," Marcy told her with a sigh. Alex, her sleeping fourteen-month-old son, was growing increasingly heavy and she shifted him from one side to the other in an effort to balance his weight. "Just say you'll come to dinner tonight."

"I'd say it," Kenzie replied willingly, "but you know I don't believe in lying." She fixed her sister with a penetrating look. "Look, Marce, I'd come over in a heartbeat if you weren't setting me up."

"Setting you up?" Marcy echoed, torn between sounding utterly innocent and completely indignant at the suggestion that she would do something so underhanded—even though that's exactly what she was doing. Her free hand was pressed against her offended breast. "Who's setting you up?" she asked, her voice cracking as it went up just a little too high at the end of her question.

"You are," Kenzie replied without blinking. Turning, she found an opening next to a vintage Singer sewing machine console and wiggled through it, leaving Marcy to lumber over to a wider aisle.

Marcy valiantly attempted to keep up the ruse. "I am not. Why would you say that?" she demanded. When Alex began to whimper in response to her elevated voice, Marcy was forced to lower it to a whisper. "Why would you say that?" she repeated in almost a hiss.

Kenzie gave her a knowing look. "You told me not to wear my jeans and to remember to fix my hair."

Because of her hectic schedule and the fact that she had to dress well for work, in her off hours Kenzie enjoyed kicking back and being comfortable during her get-togethers with her family. Apparently, in her sister's estimation, there was such a thing as being *too* comfortable.

Marcy sniffed. "I just happen to think you look nice with your hair up."

Kenzie felt compelled to point out the flaw in that excuse. "Marcy, you spend your days running after a kid whose energy levels rival the Energizer Bunny and you're about to give birth in a month or less. Why would you even *care* if I shaved my head before I came over for dinner?" she challenged. "Unless, of course," she went on, "you're inviting an extra guest to attend that dinner."

Marcy sighed, giving up the pretense. "Okay, you got me. I had Bob invite his friend George to dinner. But George is very nice—"

Kenzie immediately cut her off. This line of conversation had no future. There was no point in letting Marcy just go on and on.

"I'm sure he is," she said, patronizing Marcy just the slightest bit, "but I'm never going to find out because I'm not coming over to dinner."

Marcy looked at her pleadingly. "C'mon, Kenzie, don't be stubborn."

"You call it being stubborn. I call it surviving. Stop pulling a Mom on me," Kenzie requested, then added a little more kindly, "I have no desire to be set up. My life is full enough as it is." With that, she went on adjusting a new display of furnishings.

Marcy cast a disparaging look around at her sister's most recent acquisitions. "Yeah, full of dust and allergens," she grumbled.

Kenzie paused for a moment to pat her sister's cheek. "C'mon, Marcy. Don't pout. Your face might set that way," she teased. It was something their grandmother used to threaten them with when they were little and scowled at being reprimanded.

"What am I going to tell George?" Marcy asked. "I've already built you up to him as the greatest thing since sliced bread."

"Tell him I ran off to feed the masses," Kenzie joked. And then she sighed, shaking her head. She would have thought Marcy would know better by now. "This can't be coming as a surprise to you. You know how I feel about setups."

Marcy shifted Alex over to her other hip again, clearly physically uncomfortable. "But that's when Mom does them."

"That has nothing to do with it," Kenzie pointed out. "A setup by any other family member would be just as rotten."

Marcy played her ace card. Her eyes narrowed as she looked at her youngest sister. "You're not getting any younger, you know."

"Nobody's getting any younger, except for Brad Pitt when he played that weird guy in that movie a few years ago." Kenzie congratulated herself on delivering the comeback with a straight face.

Marcy's hands were full as she held onto her son. Otherwise she would have used one to anchor her sister and get her to agree to dinner tonight. "I'm serious, Kenzie."

"And so am I, Marce. I've got a rocking chair with my name on it at the retirement home. The second I turn thirty, I'll be sure to get my butt over there and start rocking in it."

"This isn't a joke, Kenzie," Marcy complained. She clearly wanted her sister to enjoy the sort of happiness she herself had a handle on: home, husband and an expanding family.

"Neither is being set up." Maybe if Kenzie issued a blanket warning, her siblings would cease and desist once and for all in attempting to manage her life. "Pass the word along to Marilyn. And while you're at it, you can also tell Tom and Trevor in case they're entertaining any ideas to jump in and pick up where you dropped off. *I don't want to be set up.* Got that?"

"I got it," Marcy grumbled with a sigh. "But someday, you'll regret this when you find yourself alone."

Kenzie suppressed a laugh. "Marcy, I have four married siblings with seven kids among them. I will *never* find myself alone. Besides, this way I get to be Fun Aunt Kenzie to the short tribe.

"Now please, I've got work to do and I'm going to be here all night if you don't let me finish it." She paused for a second to kiss her sleeping nephew and brush her lips against her sister's cheek. "I appreciate what you think you were doing for me, but trust me, setting me up will only lead to disaster. Now go before Pablo comes in with his duster. If you wind up staying here, you'll be sneezing for a week," she promised. "Go, Marcy."

Scowling her disapproval at the way things had turned out, Marcy murmured a few disenchanted-sounding words and then backed out of the space she was in. She was still scowling when she slowly made her way out the front door.

Kenzie breathed a sigh of relief. *Finally!*

She had exactly sixty seconds all to herself before the phone rang.

She made it to the counter, where the store phone was located, by the second ring. Managing to collect herself to convey cheerfulness, Kenzie lifted the receiver from its cradle and declared, "This is Hidden Treasures. How may I assist you today?"

The moment she heard the voice on the other end of the line, the smile she had deliberately forced to her lips widened of its own accord, generously spreading to the rest of her.

"Hello, Theresa," she said warmly to her mother's close friend and the woman who had handled several catered affairs for her. "What's up?"

It was a nice house.

Kenzie recognized it instantly. It was nothing out of the ordinary, but still very nice. And well kept.

The company her mother had founded and then passed on to her six years ago had her traveling up and down the California coast, visiting estates, regular homes and houses that fell somewhere in between. It was the middle group that tended to present her with the most surprises, yielding the occasional hidden treasure—which was why she had decided to change the shop's name to that.

Her work had taught her never to judge a book by its cover. She'd discovered that the most incredible things could be found in old cigar boxes—or their equivalent— left forgotten in the recesses of an attic, under a bed or in a seldom opened closest. Anything—from a vintage pack of playing cards once held in the hands of a famous gun- man, to a great-grandmother's precious missing cameo, to a deed to forgotten property—could turn up if some effort was given to the hunt.

What she liked most about her work was entering a different world while she assessed the belongings and, in some cases, prepared to undertake the sale of them. She always gave 110 percent of herself so her clients wound up receiving the maximum amount for their things while the items found homes with people who appreciated their worth.

Kenzie liked to call her undertaking a win-win situ- ation.

Every place, be it a simple home or an estate, had its own kind of hidden treasure, no matter how unimpres- sive that item might appear to an outsider. With that in mind, Kenzie couldn't help wondering what she would find in this pleasant residential home that Theresa Ma- netti had sent her to.

She knew it was just serendipity that brought her here because she doubted Theresa had any idea she'd once known Amy, the girl who had lived here—or that she'd had a wild crush on Amy's older brother.

Parking her car next to the curb, Kenzie got out and slowly made her way up the front walk. She did a cursory evaluation of what she saw as she went.

The property had been well maintained, although there was one hearty weed making its way up against the fence as if waiting to let loose with a growth spurt the moment no one was looking. The rest of the front yard, though, had been well tended.

The house was at the end of a cul-de-sac in an upper-class residential neighborhood. All the houses in West Park appeared to be cared for. Holding a successful estate sale here with just a little bit of advertising would require next to no effort on her part, Kenzie decided just as she reached the front door.

For a second, snatches of memories came scurrying her way, stirring questions.

*One thing at a time, Kenzie*, she told herself.

It seemed to her that the exact instant she touched the doorbell and pressed it, the front door flew open. She hoped she managed to hide her surprise from the tall, dark-haired man who answered the door.

*Oh, God, is that...?*

*Yes, it is him. Keith. This is still his house, then.*

Kenzie struggled to subdue her erratic pulse. She forced herself to breathe normally.

Had he been standing by the front window, waiting for her? Or was this just a coincidence? Mrs. Manetti had told her that according to her real estate agent friend, Maizie Sommers, the owner of this house was extremely eager to sell it and everything inside.

But somehow, until this moment, she hadn't made the

connection. She knew Keith had moved away but assumed that his mother had, too.

Because of what Mrs. Manetti had said, she should have realized this was still the O'Connell house. She supposed it was the story that threw her. Mrs. Sommers had said the seller had grown up here, which meant it was his childhood home. If anyone had told her that her parents' house was being sold, she would have been upset, not indifferent. And if she were forced to pack up whatever belongings she wanted to take with her, she would have had to hire a large moving van, not carelessly ask to have it all sold off to strangers.

But then, not everyone was as sentimental or attached to things as she was. And, she supposed, in a way there was a cloud over this house. Maybe that was what Keith had been thinking when he said he wanted everything sold.

The moment she looked up at Keith, that old queasy-stomach feeling came over her. She had to fight to keep it in check. This was business, Kenzie reminded herself. Her smile increased its wattage. Partially it was the saleswoman in her, and partially it was just the woman in her responding to the man.

He had only gotten better looking.

It figured. Was he married?

It had been ten years since she'd seen him. *Of course* he'd gotten married.

Hadn't he?

Kenzie dealt with a great many people in her line of work, and she was accustomed to all types crossing her path. As far as looks went, Keith, with his chiseled features, somber expression and sad green eyes, was definitely in the top 3 percent. She allowed her well-organized mind to wander just a little bit.

She had to admit that if Marcy or Marilyn had wanted to set her up with someone who resembled Keith, she probably wouldn't have turned the offer down, principles or no principles.

The next moment, Kenzie sternly upbraided herself for allowing her mind to wander this far off course, even for a split second. Even if it *was* Keith.

*Grow up, Kenzie.*

This was definitely *not* how she conducted business. It didn't matter if this was Keith, just as it didn't matter if she was dealing with a man who looked like Prince Charming or resembled a diseased frog. The only thing that mattered was whether or not she could help him sell the possessions inside his house. She could if those items were in decent condition or, barring that, if they were unique and interesting.

And even if that *wasn't* the case, she could offer suggestions on the measures he needed to take to make some money on the items.

All these thoughts went racing through her head in far less time than it took for an outsider to actually review what had happened.

*Showtime*, Kenzie thought. She was ready. She liked to think of herself as *always* ready.

She handed him her card. "Mr. O'Connell?" she asked, her throat feeling remarkably dry as she formally said his name. She waited for him to recognize her.

Green eyes went up and down the length of her, taking measure of her. Her breath backed up in her lungs.

"Yes?" Keith answered. There was absolutely no recognition in his eyes.

Banking down her disappointment—reminding herself that she had done a lot of transforming since she'd been in high school—Kenzie forced a smile to her lips and extended her hand to him. "Mrs. Sommers called to tell me that you were looking for someone to help you find a new home for your things."

The woman standing in front of him with the thousand-watt smile seemed far too youthful to be handling anything with the word *estate* in it. He felt as if he had just accidentally wandered into a children's story time. The underage woman made it sound as if his mother's things were animated with lives of their own.

Which was beyond ridiculous.

A distant, formless memory hovered about his brain, teasing it, but when he tried to capture it, to nail it down, it eluded him.

The woman on his doorstep reminded him of someone. Who?

He pushed the thought aside.

"Technically, they're not my things," he informed her. "I don't care if they find a home or not. I just need to get them out of the house. Mrs. Sommers seems to think the house will show much better—and sell better—if there are no distracting pieces of furniture scattered throughout the house, cluttering it up."

Kenzie nodded, hurt that there was no recognition in his eyes when he spoke to her. Reminding herself that she looked quite a bit different now didn't help.

*Give it time, Kenzie.*

"Okay," she said gamely to him once she was inside the front door. "Why don't you show me around so I can see what I've got to work with?"

He hadn't been into all the rooms since he'd returned home himself. More specifically, he hadn't seen most of the rooms since he'd left home ten years ago.

Even when he'd returned yesterday, he'd deliberately remained downstairs, sleeping on the living room sofa.

When he'd woken up after a less than restful night, he'd ventured only as far as the kitchen to make himself some breakfast.

As for the rest of the house—his room, Amy's, his mother's bedroom, the bonus room they used for a TV room—he hadn't gone into any of it. And he wanted to keep it that way until he felt up to viewing the other rooms—if that time came.

But saying anything of the kind to this woman felt far too personal.

Keith supposed he could just beg off, or murmur some noncommittal excuse that accomplished the same thing. But he had a feeling this woman wasn't the type to accept no for an answer, at least not without a really good reason.

To be fair, he decided to make one attempt at accommodating her while maintaining the balance he was searching for.

"You can just find your own way through the house. I don't mind if you poke around," he added, thinking she probably wanted a chance to review what might sell and what just needed to be carted away.

The smile was lightning fast as she attempted to coax him into accompanying her. "I'm bound to have questions," she told him. When he made no response, thinking she'd take the hint, she just continued. "If you come along as my guide, it'll go faster that way. I promise." Turning on her heel, she led the way to the staircase.

He was really beginning to regret this.

## Chapter Three

Walking ahead of him, Kenzie had just managed to climb up one step on the staircase when melodic chimes announced that there was someone on the other side of the front door.

Keith looked from the door back to the woman standing just ahead of him. He was hard-pressed to say which bothered him more—going upstairs with the woman he was still trying to place, or dealing with what had to be a prospective buyer. He wanted the house emptied almost as much as he wanted it sold. He just didn't want to be the one dealing with either firsthand.

Looking at his expression, Kenzie could almost read his mind. It occurred to her that for a relatively uncommunicative man, Keith didn't keep his thoughts all that well hidden.

"It's too soon for a prospective buyer to be turning up on your doorstep, and even if there was one this fast, he or she would be coming in with Mrs. Sommers. They

wouldn't be here on their own, ringing your doorbell—
I'm assuming you gave her a set of keys."

How had he forgotten that? Though he hated to admit
it, even to himself, all of this had shaken him up more
than he thought it would.

"Yes, I did," he answered.

As if on cue, the doorbell rang again, sounding a little more demanding this time around, if that was actually possible.

Kenzie withdrew from the first step, facing him squarely,
toe-to-toe. "I can get that for you if you'd like," she offered.

"No, thanks. I can answer it myself," he retorted stiffly,
then glanced at her expectantly.

It took her a second, but again, she seemed to sense
what he was thinking. "Why don't I just start the tour
without you?" she offered.

His grunt told her that she'd guessed right again. "That
sounds good."

Having no other recourse, Kenzie turned back around
and went up the stairs. It was only after she had reached
the landing and the doorbell had rung for a third time that
she heard any sort of movement on the floor below. Keith
was finally opening his front door.

Kenzie shook her head. She remembered a far different Keith. While not exactly gregarious, he'd been popular and friendly. What had happened to him in the past
ten years to change him into this stoic, distant man she'd
met today?

Putting Keith out of her mind, she scanned the small
bedroom she'd entered. Amy's room. Judging by the soft
decor, the pastel accent colors and the white eyelet com-
forter on the four-poster double bed, the bedroom had not
been touched since the girl had died.

Amy had been a very pretty, popular teenage girl, Kenzie recalled, looking at the photographs tacked onto the cork bulletin board above the small desk. The montage included some shots from her childhood, but for the most part, it depicted her high school years. There was even, Kenzie realized as she drew closer, a picture of Amy and her. Her heart ached a little as she looked at it. It had been taken at one of the baseball games they'd attended at school. She could remember standing next to Amy when someone had snapped it.

The next moment, another photograph caught her eye, and Kenzie paused to examine it. Amy had her arms around Keith, who appeared to be teasing her.

*That* was the Keith she remembered. A wave of nostalgia hit her. The man she'd left downstairs seemed to be light-years away from the teenager in the photograph she was looking at.

He was decidedly happier in the picture, Kenzie thought. He had laughter in his eyes. The man answering the door downstairs didn't appear as if he actually knew *how* to smile.

Kenzie swiftly took account of the closet and the other items in the room. Although the bedroom had apparently been cleaned on a regular basis, nothing had been touched or moved. It had been preserved like a shrine to Amy's memory. She guessed that had been Amy's mother's doing, because unless she'd read him incorrectly, Keith was definitely reluctant to come up here.

Had he been here since Amy's death? The thought saddened her that maybe he hadn't. Taking it a step further, she began to think that quite possibly he hadn't even been back to the house in all this time, which meant that he and his mother had been estranged at the time of her death.

Her first impulse was to run downstairs and throw her arms around him, saying how sorry she was. Of course, since he didn't seem to remember her, that would only spook him. She'd approach this more subtly, she decided—but she did intend to get to the bottom of this and find the answers to her questions. If nothing else, she owed it to Amy to see to it that Keith made peace with whatever demons were haunting him.

Kenzie went through the other two upstairs bedrooms as quickly as she could. After doing this job for a number of years, she'd developed an eye for what could sell and what would be passed over. Since Keith had told her he wanted to get rid of everything, she inventoried the clothes and furnishings, placing everything into two categories: what would sell and what would ultimately have to be disposed of in some other fashion.

When she was finished, Kenzie made her way downstairs quietly. She was just in time to hear the person—an older woman—who had rung the doorbell tell Keith, "I could drive you over to the funeral home if you'd like."

Keith guided the woman in his mother's foyer toward the door. He'd been polite, letting her elaborate on how she felt when she'd let herself into the house and found his mother unconscious on the floor, but he didn't know how much longer he could maintain his facade. He didn't want details. Details would only reel him in, and he wanted to remain distant.

It was time to send the woman on her way.

"No, I know where it is. Thanks, anyway, Mrs. Anderson."

Peggy Anderson lingered in the doorway. "It's just not going to be the same without your mother living next door to me," she told him sadly. "Your mother had a way of lighting up everyone's life the second she came in contact with them."

"So I've heard," Keith replied, an extremely tight, polite smile underscoring the words.

Observing him, Kenzie could see that he was holding himself in check. Keith was probably afraid that if he allowed his guard to go down, he'd fall apart.

Sympathy flooded through her.

It intensified as she drew closer.

Ushering Mrs. Anderson out of the house, Keith closed the door firmly behind the talkative woman. He stood there for a moment, looking at the closed door, his entire body a testimony to rigidly controlled grief.

Or so it seemed to Kenzie.

There were men who wanted only to be left alone when they were dealing with their darkest hour. However, she had never learned how to accommodate them, because everything within her cried out to offer a grieving person as much comfort as she could render.

And besides, this was Keith. There was no way she could stand on ceremony.

Coming up behind him, she placed her hand on his rigid shoulder, trying to convey her availability to comfort him in his grief. She said with a great deal of sincerity, "I'm so sorry."

Keith almost jumped when he felt her hand on his shoulder. He'd forgotten all about her. How long had she been standing there? She was supposed to be upstairs, taking inventory, not down here, eavesdropping.

He swung around to look at her. "You can't sell any of it?" Keith asked, assuming that her apology referred to the things she'd found in the upstairs bedrooms.

"What?" It took Kenzie a minute to untangle his reaction. And then she understood. They were talking about two entirely different things.

"Oh, no, I'm not apologizing about anything that has

to do with your estate. I just wanted to tell you how very sorry I am about your loss." And then Kenzie frowned, shaking her head. "The words are trite," she was quick to admit, "but that doesn't make the sentiment any less genuine."

"I'm sure it is," he said crisply, cutting the young woman off in case she had more to say on the subject.

This whole thing was much too private, and he didn't want to talk about it. However, he could see that she felt she had to say something. He shrugged away any obligation she might have thought she had in this case.

"Everyone's got to die sometime, right?" He needed to get out—and he actually did have somewhere else to be. "I have to leave for a while. Go on with your tour. Let me know if you think you can sell these things and what they might go for."

"Absolutely," she promised, then asked, "Where are you going?"

He wasn't prepared to be questioned, so he didn't have a lie on tap. Which was how the simple truth wound up coming out. "I've got to go see about making funeral arrangements."

Now there was something she'd find oppressive if she had to face it on her own. "Are you going alone?"

Again, she'd caught him off guard. And there was that weird feeling again, as if he knew her from somewhere. But that wasn't possible, was it?

Either way, Keith thought that was an odd question for her to be asking him. "Yes. Why do you ask?"

"I just thought you might want some company. You know, someone to talk to. This isn't exactly a run-of-the-mill errand you're about to undertake," she pointed out.

He turned the tables on her by saying, "If you need to talk to me, we can meet later."

With that, and a mumbled "See you later," he walked out before Kenzie had a chance to say that she thought he was the one who needed to talk, not her.

Instead of going back to her work—she had yet to inventory the first floor—Kenzie went to the front window, moved aside the curtain and stood in silence as Keith walked down the driveway to his car.

Here was someone who was either oblivious to, or more likely in denial about, the extent of his own grief.

Watching him, Kenzie made up her mind.

There were too many damn questions to answer, Keith thought wearily half an hour later.

Mrs. Anderson had told him that, per his mother's wishes, upon her death, Dorothy O'Connell wanted to be laid out at Morrison & Sons Funeral Home. He'd assumed from this information that all the paperwork had been taken care of.

He'd assumed wrong.

He supposed he could have just taken the easy way out, called the funeral director to ask about the costs and then assured the man that the check would be in the next day's mail. To be honest, Keith still wasn't entirely sure what he was doing here. It all seemed rather perverse and against what he'd always felt his role would be after his mother's final breath had been taken.

This process wasn't supposed to matter to him, but it did.

He supposed that somewhere—very deep inside—was still a sliver of the kid he had once been. The kid who had gotten along with his mother and had wanted nothing more than to take care of her and his sister. He'd wanted to be the man of the family.

He must have been all of ten or eleven years old at the time.

Before the age of reason, Keith silently added.

"I can write up a full accounting," Abe Morrison Sr. was telling him.

The funeral director looked exactly the way Keith would have expected the man to look. Tall, thin, somber, with a touch of gray at his temples and a soft voice, as if he knew that speaking above a certain decibel level would be intruding on the next-of-kin's grief.

But Keith was hardly listening to the man. He just wanted this part of it to be over with.

Hell, he wanted *all* of it to be over with.

More than anything, he wanted to be on a plane flying back to San Francisco and his life, his future, not sitting here with a stately old man, stuck in the past as he listened to him talk about a woman who was in essence a stranger to Keith and had been so for close to ten years.

Abe Morrison, however, seemed to know her very well. Why the thought irritated him so much, Keith wasn't sure, but it did and that contributed to his feelings of intense restlessness.

The man's whisper-soft voice was beginning to annoy him, as well.

"She was very explicit, your mother," Abe was saying. "She didn't want to burden you with a lot of details." A mass of wrinkles around his eyes became prominent as the funeral director offered him what appeared to be a fond smile. "Not all our clients are as thoughtful as your mother was."

Keith nodded dismissively. He didn't want to be here in this place where the dead were made to look lifelike. He took out his checkbook, hoping that would signal an end to Morrison's narrative.

Placing his checkbook on the edge of the man's mahogany desk, his pen poised, Keith asked, "So, what do I owe you?"

"Nothing," Abe replied serenely.

Keith looked up at the man. Was this some sort of a game? If it was, the point of it was lost on him. "Nothing?" he questioned.

"Nothing," Abe repeated, then went on to explain. "Your mother wrote out a check once she'd decided what she wanted. Always knew her own mind, that lady," Abe commented with just a hint of an appreciative laugh. "She prepaid her funeral expenses. She just wanted you to fill in the paperwork."

He should have known. She'd become almost flighty in that year after Amy's death, but at bottom, she was an exceedingly proud, responsible person who always insisted on paying her own way. He supposed funeral expenses were no different for her. Making him fill out the paperwork was just her way of reminding him that she was still in charge, even though she was no longer around.

Closing the checkbook again, he slipped it into his jacket's inside breast pocket. "So I guess if there's nothing further you require from me, I can be on my way."

Abe's finely curved eyebrows drew together as his brow furrowed. He gazed at Keith as if he couldn't comprehend what had just been said.

"Don't you want to view the body?" he asked, seemingly convinced that Keith hadn't really meant he wanted to leave without seeing his mother. "Our in-house cosmetic artist did an excellent job," he added quickly. "In case you think seeing her this way might be too difficult for you, I assure you that your mother just looks like she's sleeping." The lanky funeral director was already on his feet, ready to lead the way into Dorothy O'Connell's viewing room. "Come, I'll take you to the room myself. You'll be the first one to see her—other than my staff, of course."

Keith wanted to tell the man there was no need to bring him to his mother's viewing room. He wanted simply to beg off and leave. After all, he hadn't spent any time with his mother in the last ten years of her life. Why would he want to spend any time with her now that she was dead?

But he had a very strong feeling that if he left, the funeral director would only keep after him until the man got him to change his mind—or lose his temper. He might as well spare himself the aggravation. And this way, after he got this viewing over with, he'd be done with it once and for all.

So, against his better judgment, Keith allowed himself to be led into the viewing room.

He was prepared to mumble a few token words of grief for Abe Morrison's benefit and then leave the funeral home and this part of his past once and for all.

What Keith *wasn't* prepared for was that the funeral director would leave him alone in the viewing room.

And he definitely wasn't prepared for the impact that being alone with his mother's body would have on him. Logically, he knew it wasn't her. It was just the empty shell of what had once *been* his mother.

And yet…

She still seemed to be right there, a part of everything. A part of him.

Keith felt as if someone had stolen the breath out of his lungs, then sat on his chest, daring him to suck air back in.

He couldn't.

For just a second, before he regained control over himself, Keith thought he was going to black out.

"Guess you got in the last word, after all, didn't you?" he asked his mother, the question barely above a whisper.

Keith felt tears gathering in the corners of his eyes, and he damned himself for it and her for making him have to go through this.

"This doesn't change anything, you know," he told her gruffly. "This death thing isn't going to soften me and make me decide you were right and I was wrong. I wasn't wrong. *You* were. Wrong to act like life was one great big party, wrong to act like you were a teenager, living life to the fullest—and more.

"I know what you were trying to do," he told the still form lying in the blue silk–lined casket. "You were trying to live Amy's life for her after she couldn't live it herself. But you couldn't do that," he pointed out, the very words he uttered scraping against the inside of his throat. "Nobody gets to live someone else's life. Everybody's got one chance to live, and if that's taken away, well, then it's gone."

He leaned over the casket just a tad, bringing his face in closer to hers. Damn it, the funeral director was right. She *did* look as if she were sleeping.

He felt as if Death—and his mother—were rubbing his nose in the fact that she was gone.

"There are no do-overs, even if you thought there should be. *You* don't get to decide things like that," he informed her. And then his voice grew louder as his anger came to the fore. "Don't you think it tore me apart, seeing you do that? Acting like Amy when Amy wasn't there anymore? You were her mother—*my* mother. You were supposed to act like one, not like some teenage girl with a mission.

"And where did all that get you in the end?" he demanded heatedly. "Nowhere, dead on a slab, that's where it got you." Because now that he thought about it, his mother's erratic, age-denying lifestyle must have contributed to her demise. "Now your life's gone, too, just like Amy's."

The disgust abated from his voice, and it softened again just a hint. "Maybe you could have lived longer if you hadn't lived so crazy. I don't know, and it's too late to find out." He turned to leave, then stopped, another wave of recrimination hovering on his lips. "But you shouldn't have done it. You shouldn't have," he repeated, stopping short of raising his voice to the level of shouting.

He didn't want to attract anyone to the room. Having a meltdown here in the middle of the funeral home was bad enough without it being witnessed by a bunch of strangers.

Still, Keith stood there in the room for a few more moments, doing his best to pull himself together. Searching for a way to reconcile the fact that he was never going to see his mother's face again. This was to be the last time he'd see her, and he told himself that he shouldn't care.

But he did.

Calling himself a fool, Keith squared his shoulders and turned to walk out of the small viewing room. He didn't have time for this, didn't have time to let something as useless as grief eat away at him. He had loose ends to tie up and a busy life to get back to. He wouldn't stand around and mope over a woman who had had no regard for him whatsoever, who had shut him out when he'd tried to reach her and make her accept reality.

This, he thought, taking one last look at Dorothy O'Connell, was the final reality.

Turning, he took a long stride out of the room—and walked straight into the young woman he couldn't quite place, who was standing just outside the room.

And who was apparently, if the expression on her face and the tears glistening in her eyes were any indication, listening to every word he'd just said to his late mother.

## Chapter Four

It was a toss up whether he was more surprised or angry to find her there.

"Please tell me you've found a buyer for all those things in the house. Either that, or you suddenly need a funeral home, because otherwise, you have absolutely no reason to be here right now, hovering outside my mother's viewing room," he informed her.

He wasn't all that sure he could tolerate the truth, but he wasn't about to put up with any kind of lie.

"You're my reason," she told him, her voice as quiet as his was sharp.

*Stalker.*

The word flashed through his head in big, bold letters. Was that what he'd done, hired a stalker? The possibility made him angrier.

The scowl on his face was meant to be intimidating. "You're going to have to explain that. Carefully," he warned.

His eyes held her prisoner, as if to say that he could see right through her and would immediately know if she was lying to him.

Because he seemed so angry, Kenzie deliberately curbed her habit of speaking quickly. Instead, she enunciated every word that she uttered so he could absorb it.

"You were coming here alone, and this isn't the sort of thing a person should have to face alone," she told Keith with feeling. "I thought you might need a friend, so I came."

Keith stared at her. "You're not my friend. We have a working relationship," he reminded her tersely, then added, "I don't make friends that easily."

That she could readily believe, despite how popular he'd once been. Still, even though he had apparently changed, that didn't alter the way she felt about what he was going through or what had initially compelled her to come to the funeral home, looking for him.

Given what she'd heard him say when he thought no one was listening, she knew better than most what he was going through.

Kenzie approached the subject slowly. "I had an argument with my father."

Keith's scowl deepened. "I'm not your priest, either, which means I don't do confessions." And then his curiosity about what she was thinking got the better of him. "What does your argument with your father have to do with me?" he demanded.

Kenzie pretended that he hadn't asked any impatient questions. Instead, she went on as if the man she addressed was quietly waiting to be enlightened.

"My father definitely had opinions about my lifestyle, my choice of friends. You know, all the usual reasons fathers and daughters butt heads. I put up with it for a while, then decided that if that was how he felt, it was his loss, not mine, and I stopped talking to him. I refused to return his calls and, to make a long story short—"

"Too late," Keith informed her tersely.

He was making it difficult for her to get her point across, but she pushed on. "I smugly put him in his place— or so I thought." Her voice became more serious as she continued. "I also thought there was all the time in the world to resolve these differences between us when I was good and ready to."

Kenzie took a breath. She and her father had had more than their share of differences, but she'd loved him, and it still hurt to think about him no longer being part of her life.

"My father died before that happened. To this day, I really regret not mending those fences. And I regret not getting off my high horse and just declaring those differences we had to be meaningless water under the bridge." She looked up into Keith's eyes. "So I know firsthand what it's like to have someone die on you before you have a chance to make up."

"I had no intentions of making up," he informed Kenzie.

Kenzie shook her head. "You say that now, but you don't really mean it."

"Look—"

Kenzie wasn't about to back down from her position. She was certain that she was right and he was in a state of stubborn denial.

"No one but the Tasmanian Devil wants to live in a state of perpetual warfare." She looked past Keith's shoulder toward the casket. "I'd like to pay my last respects to your mother."

That *really* didn't make any sense to him. "Why would

you possibly want to look at the earthly remains of Dorothy O'Connell?"

Moving into the room, Kenzie gazed down at the woman and then at Keith before turning back to the deceased again. "I'm looking at more than that."

"An estate sale with a side order of philosophy," Keith said sarcastically. "Does that come as a package deal, or am I required to pay extra for it?"

"You know," she said in a tone that was devoid of judgment and composed solely of concern, "you might do a lot better getting along with yourself if you just dropped the attitude—and the 'philosophy,' as you call it, is free. As for our business arrangement, I only get a percentage of the total sales once they're final," she pointed out. "That's written in the contract I brought with me," she told him before he had a chance to ask about it.

Circumventing him, Kenzie went straight to the casket for a closer look at his mother. "She was always a pretty lady," she observed softly. Her mouth curved a little as she added, "She looks so young."

He shrugged, telling himself he didn't care about his mother, about any of it. "That was her goal."

His retort was cynical. Kenzie raised her eyes to his. When had his soul become so tortured? she couldn't help thinking.

"Everyone deals with grief in their own way." Her comment had him eyeing her quizzically. "I heard you talking to her," she told him, thinking it was best not to elaborate any further right now.

"Of course you did," he responded. She could tell he struggled to curb his annoyance.

She watched his expression as she said, "I was just trying to help."

"You want to help?" he retorted. "Don't eavesdrop.

Don't follow me. Just sell the damn things in the house. That's all I need or want from you."

He needed more than that, Kenzie couldn't help thinking, even if he didn't consciously realize it. But for now, she pretended to go along with his instructions and nodded her head.

"I still have to go over some of the inventory with you."

He'd hired her at the agent's suggestion so he *wouldn't* have to deal with any of that. Now she seemed determined to pull him in to do exactly what he didn't want to do.

"Why?"

"So I can put a proper price on the items," she replied innocently. She had more of a motive than that—she wanted to help him deal with his feelings and the past— but saying so would only accomplish the exact opposite.

"Isn't that up to you?" he asked. "You're supposed to be the one with the expertise in vintage clutter."

He was hiding behind insults, but she had an idea that wasn't how he felt about it, not really, not deep down.

"I'd need you to point out the items that have more sentimental value for you—"

Keith immediately cut her short. "Well, that's easy enough. There aren't any."

The house was filled with clothes, photographs and other things. It seemed impossible to her that he didn't have at least a few favorite items amid the rest.

"None?" she asked.

His answer was firm. "None."

Kenzie studied him for a long moment. "I don't believe you."

"Believe me or not. I really don't care *what* you believe. All I want from you is to deal with the facts as they exist."

When it came to battles, Kenzie had learned that picking the time and place gave her some advantage. For now she acquiesced. "If you say so."

His eyes narrowed. "I say so."

His voice was firm, but Keith didn't believe what she'd just said for an instant. This woman didn't strike him as the type to withdraw suddenly like that. Even after only a couple of hours, she seemed a bit more of a fighter than that. If he were to put a bet on it, he'd say the woman was a great example of sneak attacks and most likely was the human personification of guerrilla warfare.

Kenzie pressed on in her own fashion. "I'd still take it as a favor if you would give me some sort of a bottom-line price on some of the things I found in your mother's closet."

Keith grunted something unintelligible in response as they left the funeral home. He had no desire to go through the things in his mother's closet.

Kenzie turned toward him once they were outside in the parking lot and asked, completely out of the blue, "When's the funeral?"

There was nothing boring about this woman, Keith thought. "In three days. My mother, according to Mrs. Anderson and confirmed by the funeral director, left very specific instructions as to what she wanted. She thought three days would give all her friends enough time to say goodbye." He was reiterating what the director had told him.

It was obvious to Kenzie that he did not appreciate the time frame. Stepping over to the side, she tried to put what he seemed to view as an ordeal in a more flattering light.

"That was very thoughtful of her."

He, apparently, didn't see it that way.

"Or vain," Keith countered. "Think what it says for her to believe she has enough friends that they would fill up three days of a calendar. I don't know of anyone short of a Hollywood celebrity who could have that sort of a following."

What had made him so bitter? Kenzie wondered. There had to be something else at work here, not just an estrangement between a mother and her son. Had Amy's death been the trigger?

"Oh, I don't know," she told him. "I'd like to think that people who touch other people's lives on a regular basis might get that kind of a send-off when their time comes. Your mother obviously meant a lot to many people."

Keith studied her for a moment before turning away and going to his car.

This woman his agent had recommended was definitely a Pollyanna type, he thought disparagingly. Just his luck. The last person he wanted in his life right now was Pollyanna.

He made an attempt to set her straight, admittedly more for his sake than hers. There was just so much cheerfulness and optimism he could put up with listening to, and he was past his limit.

"People aren't nearly as nice as you seem to think they are," he told her.

"And," Kenzie interjected, "they're not nearly as evil, self-centered and hot-tempered as you seem to think they are." The look she gave him said they were at a stalemate and for now, she was willing to let it go at that.

"Better safe than sorry," he pointed out.

She pressed her lips together, aware that since he was the client and she was in essence working for him, she should just drop this.

And she did.

For about five seconds.

"Being safe is highly overrated," she told him.

Kenzie paused for a moment, back to debating whether or not to reveal who she was. Initially, she'd decided not to mention it, but as things began to progress, she'd gotten more and more tempted to let him in on the truth.

She decided to begin slowly and see where this went. "You know, it's okay for you to grieve. People will understand."

"What they won't understand is *not* grieving," he pointed out, then shrugged as he added, "But, well, you can't show what you don't feel, right?"

"I don't believe that," she told him quietly. His comment didn't jibe with what she knew about him, or had once known, at any rate.

Keith was about to tell her that he didn't care what she believed or didn't believe. But he never got the chance, because she went on to say with more conviction than he felt she should exhibit, "Your mother was a very special lady."

Keith sorely disliked people preaching on things they couldn't possibly have any idea about. "And you came to this conclusion how?" he demanded. "By standing and looking at her for a total of, oh, about sixty seconds?"

"No, it was a lot longer than that."

There was contempt in his eyes. "Maybe you'd better learn how to tell time."

Okay, now she had to tell him the rest of it, Kenzie decided. The moment she'd recognized him and realized who he was, she'd wavered on whether or not to tell him right off the bat. But he'd been so removed, so distant, she'd decided there was no point in saying anything. He might even be suspicious why she'd bring this into their dealings. But now she didn't see how she could avoid it.

"I don't have any trouble telling time," she informed him.

Keith ushered her impatiently over to the far edge of

the sidewalk, away from the funeral home's entrance.
"What are you talking about?" he asked.

She took a breath before beginning, then plunged in.
She began with the most obvious line. "You don't remember me, do you?"

"Remember you?" Keith repeated, confused. Okay,
something familiar about her had been nagging at him,
but she had no way of knowing that. "You came to my
door this afternoon, saying that my agent sent you. I admit
I'm out of my depth here, but my memory's not exactly
Swiss cheese. I remember you from this afternoon."

She made no comment on his response. Instead, she
went straight to the part he needed to hear. "We went to
school together."

His eyes narrowed as he focused on her face. "'We' as
in you and I?" he questioned suspiciously.

She nodded, then added, "And Amy."

Kenzie watched as her client's face darkened. She
could tell that he thought she was making this up. That
for some perverse reason, she was using his sister to get
him to trust her or open up to her.

Nothing could have been further from the truth.

"I don't remember you," he told her in a low, somber
and dismissive voice. He meant for it to terminate the
conversation before it went any further.

But it didn't.

"I was in Amy's homeroom and a few of her classes.
We were friendly." She could see that he still didn't believe her—most likely because he still didn't recognize
her. In an odd way, she took that as a compliment. It had
taken her a long while to learn how to play up her assets,
how to style her hair and perform all the other small tricks
that it took to make a silk purse out of what had been, in
her opinion, a sow's ear.

Taking out her phone, Kenzie began to flip through something on the bottom of her screen.

"Are you planning on calling someone to back you up?" Keith asked.

"No, I thought this might jar your memory a little—not that we exchanged more than about five or six words in high school." It had been the classic scenario. "You were the sophisticated senior at the time, and I was the klutzy sophomore."

What she was flipping through were the photographs on her phone. Most of that space was devoted to the merchandise she had acquired and was attempting to sell in her store.

But in addition to those photographs, she also had a good many photographs of her family. And she had made it a point to have one photograph of herself in that collection. The photograph captured the way she looked back in high school. She kept it to remind her never to allow herself just to coast along. Appearance, success and everything in between required constant work.

Settling for a status quo eventually led to failure.

"This was me in high school." Turning her phone around, she held it up for his perusal. "Now do you remember me?"

He'd only meant to glance at it and dismiss what she was saying. But the second he looked down at the screen on her phone, a memory began to stir within the recesses of his mind.

The distant memory that been elusively playing hide-and-seek with his brain was back again. He stared at the photo for a handful of minutes—and then the light bulb went off in his head. Stunned, he looked at her in disbelief.

"You're Clumsy Mac."

The wince was automatic. She hadn't heard that name in years and would have thought she had risen above re-acting to it.

Obviously not.

"Not the most flattering nickname, but yes," Kenzie admitted, "I was called that."

Taking the phone from her, Keith stared at the screen, then looked back at her before looking down at the photograph again.

There was only one word that was applicable here. "Wow."

Kenzie's generous mouth curved. "I'll take that as a compliment."

He hardly heard what she said. He was having a great deal of trouble believing that Clumsy Mac and the woman standing before him were one and the same person. He asked the obvious.

"Did you have surgery done?"

She tried not to pay attention to the fact that his question could be taken as an insult. She sensed he hadn't meant it that way, which was all that counted.

"Actually, no. This is the result of a good hair stylist and learning how to use makeup."

"Learning?" he echoed. "I think you graduated," he murmured, looking back at the person captured on her mobile phone.

The difference between that teenager and the woman standing in front of him was like night and day—and, in his opinion, nothing short of a miracle.

## Chapter Five

Keith wasn't sure how he felt about the idea that he knew the person handling the so-called "estate" sale of the furnishings and other items within his mother's house.

In recent years he'd come to feel that there was something to be said for anonymity. Since he and Kenzie had, in a manner of speaking, a vague sort of history together, he had an uneasy feeling that he was leaving himself open to an invasion of privacy somewhere down the road. He had little doubt that Kenzie would believe their having attended the same high school entitled her to ask questions and be on a familiar footing with him, whereas if they were actually strangers, he would be able to keep her at a distance more easily.

He was overthinking this, he told himself. After all, MacKenzie Bradshaw was a professional, and he sincerely doubted that his agent would have suggested her for the job if Kenzie wasn't up to getting the job done— and more than just adequately.

Besides, he wouldn't have to put up with any of this for long. He was flying back to San Francisco the second the funeral was over. His presence here certainly wasn't necessary for the sale of either the house or the things that were in it. That was why he'd come to Maizie Sommers to begin with.

Sanctuary would be his very shortly, Keith promised himself—provided, of course, that he survived the next few days. There were times that he wasn't sure of the inevitability of that outcome.

In a bid for simplicity and moving things along at an acceptable pace, Keith had reconsidered checking into a hotel as he'd planned after the first night. He'd grown up in this house, he reasoned, so he could endure staying here for a few more days rather than commuting back and forth from the hotel, braving traffic and steep hotel rates.

Ever practical, he saw no reason to complicate matters and have to pay premium prices just for a place to sleep, which was all that his stay at a hotel would have amounted to. The rest of his time while he was in Bedford would be spent either fielding Kenzie's free-flowing questions or being involved in myriad details connected to his mother's funeral.

He discovered that he didn't have to tackle them alone if he didn't want to. Kenzie proved to be good at not just her job but also a whole host of other things. Like deciphering what amounted to illegible handwriting in his opinion.

When she found him in the living room less than an hour after they returned to the house, he was frowning over the unreadable entries in his mother's worn little red address book. Kenzie was *not* shy about asking him what was wrong.

Kenzie was not shy about *anything*.

He didn't bother hiding that he was less than happy about whatever needed doing next. "I'm going to have to call my mother's friends to let them know where and when the funeral service will be held."

Kenzie apparently picked up on his reluctance. "Would you like me to call them for you?"

For just a moment, he allowed himself to savor the wave of relief that washed over him. He was more than willing to have her take over this tedious, not to mention uncomfortable, chore.

But the next moment, reality set in, as it always did. "And say what?" he asked. "That you're my administrative assistant and you're making these calls about Dorothy O'Connell's passing on the behalf of the only family she has left?"

Kenzie inclined her head, indicating her basic agreement with his assessment. "That would be the gist of it, although not exactly in those words." In her opinion, he'd sounded not just detached but also a tad sarcastic, neither of which would work in this situation once he started calling and talking to his mother's friends. "I thought all lawyers knew how to charm juries."

Keith frowned again as he looked down at the page he'd opened the book to. "The people in this book aren't a jury," he pointed out.

Okay, so her choice of words left something to be desired. "Maybe not, but the charm thing can still work. Besides, juries are comprised of people, and these *are* people you'll be calling," Kenzie said, indicating the address book.

Keith sighed, frustrated. "Illegible people." He shook his head. "My mother had the world's worst handwriting. A chicken with its beak dipped in ink could write more legibly than my mother did." And that was being charitable. "For all I know, this could be an annotated list of a herd of ponies," he grumbled, waving the address book.

"May I?" Kenzie held out her hand toward him, her indication clear. She wanted him to surrender the book to her so she could see firsthand what she would be up against.

Keith gladly surrendered the cause of his eyestrain and blossoming headache. "Be my guest. And if you can read any of those names and numbers, I'll buy you a filet mignon dinner."

The grin Kenzie gave him told Keith how game she was even before she said, "You're on."

Kenzie skimmed down the first couple of pages quickly before she raised her eyes to his again. She fixed Keith with a mesmerizing look he found almost too hypnotic. Drawing his eyes away proved to be a real problem— which in turn annoyed him. He didn't need extraneous thoughts right now.

"What restaurant?" she asked him, the grin still playing along her lips.

He looked at her sharply. She had to be bluffing. "You're kidding."

"Frequently," Kenzie allowed. "Going along with the popular belief, laughter really *is* the best medicine. However," she went on, "I'm not kidding this time. Would you like me to type these names and numbers up for you?" she offered.

"You can read them?" he asked in disbelief.

"Absolutely," she told him without hesitation.

For a moment, he was going to accuse her of lying, but why would she lie? She had to know he'd call her on it, and she obviously was ready to back up her claim by recreating the entries.

Getting up, he circled around her until he was looking over her shoulder at the same page she was.

*Incredible*, he thought.

"Do you want me to write them down?" she offered again, prodding him for an answer.

He wouldn't have use for any of those names once the people listed in it were notified.

"No need," he told her. "As long as they know the date, time and location of the funeral—"

"And the reception," she added. Didn't he realize that there was always some sort of a reception held after a funeral?

Obviously not, she thought, judging by the blank expression on Keith's face when he looked at her. "What reception?"

Kenzie gave him the benefit of the doubt. Maybe the man had never been to a funeral before. "The one you're going to be holding for everyone after your mother's funeral."

"No, I'm not. I'm not holding anything. I'm flying back to San Francisco right after the funeral," he told her firmly.

"Are you expecting some sort of an emergency?" Kenzie questioned innocently.

He saw right through her and it irritated him, but there was no point in letting her see that. After all, she was just trying to help here. But he could be honest with her.

"The emergency is that I can't take being here for any length of time."

Kenzie very politely shot down his plans for an early escape. "Hold a reception," she told him. "Trust me, you'll regret it if you don't. It doesn't take all that much to throw a reception together if you know the right people to ask." That she knew such people went without saying. "Your mother's friends will expect it."

"I'm never going to see any of these people again. Why should it matter to me what they think?"

She refrained from pointing out the obvious—he would be doing it to honor his mother, and that sort of thing was expected. Instead, she tried to appeal to his practical side.

"Call it tying up loose ends. You'll feel better about it when you look back."

For a relative stranger—despite their common background—Kenzie Bradshaw seemed awfully confident that she knew how he'd react to something when he would have occasion to look back on it someday in the future. He almost called her on it, then decided there was no point.

Besides, he needed all the help he could get, and for whatever reason, this woman seemed perfectly content to handle all this for him.

"Okay, we'll have the reception." Then he tapped the edge of the tattered address book. "Now see what you can do with this."

She flipped over to a few more pages in the same worn condition. "Do you want everyone in the address book notified about your mother's funeral and reception?"

He shrugged. On his own, he wouldn't have known who to call and who to leave out. "Might as well." And then he thought of one restriction. "Just the people who are located in the States."

He was not about to postpone the entire funeral service just because someone couldn't make immediate travel arrangements. This was already getting too drawn out.

Kenzie nodded. "Understood."

Holding on to the tattered address book, Kenzie sat down and made herself comfortable on the sofa. She took out her cell phone.

"You can use the house phone," Keith told her. He had no idea who her carrier was or what data plan she had.

She was essentially doing him a favor, and he didn't want it costing her anything on top of that.

"This is fine," Kenzie assured him. "Besides, the house phone won't reach over here." She pointed to the landline, which was located on the kitchen wall, and smiled as she said, "Your mother didn't appear to be a supporter of cordless phones."

He hadn't taken any notice of that. Now that he did, Keith laughed shortly. "I guess some things never change," he commented. The phone in the kitchen looked as if it was the same one that had been there when he still lived at home.

Just for a glimmer of a moment, she thought she saw nostalgia flash in Keith's eyes. She wanted to ask him about it, but she instinctively knew where that would lead. Keith wasn't ready to talk. She could see that. Whether this involved unresolved issues between Keith and his mother or something else, he'd have to approach it slowly, in stages, not all at once like a firestorm. And right now, he had trusted her enough to ask for help.

That was step one.

"I'd better get started," Kenzie told him as she opened the address book and turned to the first page, her cell phone ready in her other hand.

Taking his cue, Keith left her to it.

Or thought he did.

The problem was that the house was so quiet, it was almost eerie. There was no competing noise to draw his attention away from the sound of Kenzie's voice as she made call after call, saying, essentially, the same thing over and over again.

Even with a room between them—he was in the tiny room that had been used as a study—he could still hear her clearly.

Kenzie's voice, he thought, sounded almost melodic despite the fact that it was infused with the proper subdued decorum as she called the first of many people to announce solemnly his mother's passing.

He caught himself being drawn to the sound of her voice even though he tried not to listen.

He fully expected Kenzie to keep her end of the conversation identical from call to call. But after listening to her phone what he assumed were the first two people in the book, he realized she was tailoring what she said.

Kenzie Bradshaw was nothing if not personable. He found himself admiring her.

He had spent the first night here on the sofa rather than going upstairs to his old bedroom. But with the sound of Kenzie's voice filling up the living room and perforce the surrounding area, he decided he needed to escape. So he reluctantly went upstairs to his room, thinking he'd give what he'd left there ten years ago a cursory look on the off chance that there actually *was* something he might want to keep from that period of his life.

As he climbed up the stairs, Keith couldn't help thinking that he'd lucked out hiring Kenzie. What she was doing right now was definitely over and above the call of duty. He appreciated that she had taken on what would have been to him nothing short of an ordeal. Notifying people that someone they knew and presumably liked was dead was an onerous task. That went double since the deceased was his mother.

Yet Kenzie had taken the job on more than willingly.

He wondered why she'd done that.

Was she playing some sort of an angle? And if so, what?

He'd been a lawyer much too long. Otherwise, he wouldn't be on his guard like this. Not everyone had an underhanded motive in mind, he reminded himself. Sometimes a kindness was just a kindness.

The embroidery-worthy slogan caught him up short as it popped into his head.

That was something his mother used to say. Now that he thought about it, she had always been a champion of good deeds for their own sake, not for any sort of financial gain or reward other than a feeling of satisfaction.

And then he frowned, remembering that their last argument had been about just that.


A strong feeling of déjà vu swept over Keith the moment he crossed the threshold into his old bedroom. Until this point, he had been convinced he was in no danger of feeling even remotely nostalgic. After all, he'd left in the heat of anger, and anger had continued to be his shield all these years.

When he thought of the house on Normandie, there was no overwhelming fondness vying for his attention. There was just that feeling of anger, anger that effectively managed to cocoon him.

So where was that shield, that cocoon now? he silently demanded.

Keith felt naked and exposed, and he definitely felt vulnerable.

He almost turned on his heel and walked out again, but that would have been cowardly and he refused to be a coward, even if only in his own eyes.

So he forced himself to remain in the room, opening bureau drawers and looking into his closet.

Much to his frustration, the feeling of nostalgia refused to abate. It grew. Grew until he could feel it emanating from every corner, from every nook in his room.

Even looking at his high school jacket, the one with the

letter he'd been so proud of, wound up being another occasion for nostalgia to ambush him. It happened not just when he put it on but also when he slipped his hands into the pockets. He expected them to be empty.

They weren't.

His fingers in his right pocket came in contact with something soft. When he pulled it out, he found it was a ribbon. For a moment, he stared at it, unable to remember whom it belonged to.

And then he remembered all too well. His stomach tightened.

The ribbon had belonged to Amy. It had come undone from her hair and she'd lost it. He'd found the ribbon, and out of habit, he picked it up. Amy was always losing things. Ribbons, schoolbooks, those funny little dangling earrings she loved so much. He'd teased her, saying that with her penchant for losing things, she was lucky to have kept her clothes on.

Trying to shake off the feeling, he shoved the ribbon back into his pocket and stripped the jacket off. He threw it into the bottom of his closet and quickly closed the sliding closet door, as if hiding it from view could somehow erase the feeling he was experiencing.

It didn't.

Kenzie chose that moment to come walking in. "It's done," she announced.

His mind still elsewhere, Keith looked at her uncomprehendingly.

"I called all the people in your mother's book." To say that it had been a grueling ordeal would have been an understatement. But no one had forced her to do it. She'd volunteered, she reminded herself, so she had no right to complain. "Everyone is profoundly sorry to hear about your mother's passing. They had some really nice things to say about her. It might have been good for you to hear," she couldn't help telling him. "I jotted some of the things down if you want to see for yourself."

She held the pad she'd used out to him.

Keith deliberately ignored the pad. Rather than accept it, he just shrugged. "I'll take your word for it." He got back to the only thing that mattered here as far as he was concerned. "So it's done?"

"The notification part, yes. It's done."

"What other part is there?" he asked, then realized what she was probably referring to. "Oh, you mean attending the funeral."

"Actually, I was referring to the arrangements for the reception."

The reception. He was hoping she'd forgotten about that. He should have known better.

"Yeah, about that. There're too many details to see to at this late date. I don't think that I can—"

"But I can," she interjected, reminding him of what she'd said earlier. "I'll handle it for you," she volunteered.

She was turning into his own personal valet, and he had to admit, he really did appreciate the help. But he had to draw the line at this. There was such a thing as abusing an offer of help, no matter how willing she seemed to be.

"It's too much," he maintained stubbornly.

She glossed right over his protest.

"We can hold it here—after all, this is where all of your mother's friends were probably accustomed to coming. The house has that kind of warmth to it," she added when he looked at her quizzically. "And the reception doesn't have to be anything fancy. All it has to do is *be*," she stressed.

And then she tackled the biggest obstacle that he could raise before he had a chance to do it. "I happen to know someone who could cater this for you at a more than reasonable price," she promised, thinking of Mrs. Manetti.

Okay, this was getting into the realm of being too good to be true—which meant that it ultimately wasn't. Somewhere down the line, there had to be a catch.

"So, aside from selling vintage furnishings, you moonlight as what—a magician, is that it?" Keith asked almost accusingly.

"No," she told him, doing her best not to pay attention to his skeptical tone. "I just happen to have a lot of connections."

*I just bet you do*, Keith couldn't help thinking. Anyone who looked the way this woman did undoubtedly had *lots* of connections.

# Chapter Six

In the end, though it was against his better judgment, Keith gave in and told this woman who had popped up out of his past to go ahead with the arrangements for the reception.

It was proving to be easier to say yes than to argue with Kenzie. To the casual observer, she might appear to be incredibly easygoing, but obviously in this case looks not only could be deceiving but also actually were.

The enterprising young woman was tenacious. *Extremely* tenacious. Keith quickly discovered that when she thought she was right about something, Kenzie just dug in. He had a feeling that if he didn't tell her to go ahead with the reception, she would keep chipping away at him until he finally gave in.

This way spared him a lot of useless grief.

What actual business this was of hers he had yet to figure out, but since his mother's friends did seem to expect there would be a reception held after the funeral and

Kenzie was willing to make all the arrangements for him, he figured there was no point in fighting it.

He supposed it was, in essence, a win-win situation—except that he didn't actually want a reception after the funeral in the first place...

But then, he really didn't want to have to go through with the funeral service, either. However, there was just no way around it.

The situation he found himself facing made him think of one of the senior partners at his law firm, Nathan Greeley. Greeley had a large family, and one or more of them were always giving the man grief. He'd once asked Greeley how he put up with it. The senior partner had told him he just threw money at the problem until it finally went away.

At the time, he'd thought the response seemed like a rather cold—not to mention wasteful—philosophy. But he could fully appreciate the man's thinking right now. He could also readily embrace it now that he was dealing with Kenzie and his mother's funeral.

Keith supposed that, in all honesty, he couldn't really complain. Kenzie was actually doing the work. He just had to pay the bills.

For the second time, he couldn't help thinking that he had certainly gotten more than he'd bargained for by hiring Kenzie.

In more ways than one.

She was definitely a far cry from the awkward, unsure teenager he only vaguely remembered from high school.

But then, to be fair, he supposed that *he* was a far cry from the person he had been back then, as well.

Shrugging, Keith pushed any further examination of those years aside. It served no purpose. He was who he was.

*A man without a family.*

The thought just seemed to pop up in his head out of nowhere. Jagged and painful in its brutal simplicity, it proved to be hard to push aside.

The funeral, and everything that was associated with it, was supposed to have been just a sidebar. The sale of the house and its furnishings were supposed have taken center stage for him until they were effectively history for him, as well.

But things weren't progressing nearly as swiftly as he would have liked. It felt as if the sale was on temporary hold until after the funeral and reception were over.

He wasn't quite sure how that had happened. Kenzie had mentioned something to him in passing that postponing putting the house up for sale was just showing the proper respect for his mother. He'd been tempted to say that his mother never bothered showing him any proper respect, but he bit his tongue and refrained.

The funeral would be held in three days, and he supposed he could wait until then.

Besides, mercifully, Kenzie seemed to be really invested in making all the arrangements. To her credit—if he could call it that—she did try to pull him into every decision, but he kept abdicating his position and telling her to do what she felt was best—as long as it remained simple.

Even so, Kenzie kept trying.

She even came to him with a choice of three different menus for the reception.

He was on the sofa at the time, trying to distract himself by finding something vaguely entertaining on television. Never an avid viewer, he was striking out rather badly.

Armed with printed material, Kenzie bent over the coffee table and spread out the menus for him to review.

"What looks good to you?" she asked.

Keith glanced away from the set and looked in her direction. The first thing he noticed wasn't any of the menus she'd laid out for him. It was the way her light blue blouse dipped down, allowing him to glimpse just the slightest hint of cleavage—only enough to distract him—as she fussed over the menus.

As if his brain was on some delayed timer, when he realized what he was doing—and that she was looking at him—Keith said the first thing that came to mind that didn't include her.

Or food, for that matter.

Clearing his throat, he muttered, "A shot of vodka comes to mind."

Kenzie effortlessly took his response in stride, incorporating it in her answer. "There'll be a bar for those who feel the need for something a little more bracing than soda." Straightening up as unobtrusively as possible when she realized that her neckline had dipped down, Kenzie tapped an index finger once on each of the menus. "I meant, which of these menus do you want at the reception?"

None stood out from the other two. They looked equally acceptable. Keith waved a dismissive hand at the array. "It doesn't matter."

The look he caught her giving him in response said that it did matter.

"Okay, you pick," he told Kenzie, adding for her benefit, "I defer to your judgment. You seem to be in tune to what these women want."

She couldn't help wondering if Keith knew how aloof he sounded. She refused to believe he really felt that way. There was a human being underneath all that. She was sure of it. He couldn't have changed all that much from the person she remembered when she'd had that massive crush on him in high school.

"What they want is the opportunity to get together and trade favorite stories about your mother. And what I want," she added quietly, catching him by surprise, "is for you not to patronize me."

Keith frowned. He hadn't realized that he'd allowed his facade to slip down. He was usually a lot better at keeping his mask in place when dealing with a distasteful situation.

"I wasn't patronizing you," he protested.

Kenzie laughed dryly and rolled her eyes.

"Oh, please. I'm an optimist, not an idiot. You're angry. I get it. But eventually, the anger's going to pass. If you don't do this, if you just turn your back on your mother, her friends and everything else, you're going to regret it. And regret has amazing staying power. It has a tendency to haunt us for a very long time."

He doubted that Kenzie had ever regretted anything in her whole life. He, on the other hand, did. And that was what he was attempting to deal with right now.

"More philosophy?" he asked flippantly.

"Call it whatever you like. And no, it's not part of a package deal. It's on the house," she added with a tolerant, lopsided smile.

With that, she scooped the menus up off the coffee table and began to walk out of the room.

The woman was trying, and he shouldn't be making it this hard for her. With an inward sigh, he called out to her. "Kenzie?"

Kenzie paused, then glanced at him over her shoulder. "Yes?"

"Which one did you decide on?"

"The one with chicken. There are people who have issues with beef or pork, but almost everyone likes chicken," she told him.

It made sense, and Keith nodded. Just as she did cross the threshold, he added what he'd left unsaid. "Thanks for doing this."

Again, she looked at Keith over her shoulder and smiled. "No problem," she assured him.

And she sounded like she actually meant it.

It was the smell of coffee that woke him the next morning.

At first, as the aroma wafted into the misty domain comprising his dormant, unconscious state, Keith was sure he was just dreaming.

But he could still smell the strong aroma when he opened his eyes.

What the…?

He was certain that he hadn't set the coffee machine on a timer. Last night came back to him, and he remembered watching *Executive Decision*, a favorite movie he must have seen at least twenty times, if not more. Flipping channels, he'd encountered it—a few scenes into the story—on one of the cable stations, and it was like running into an old friend.

Watching it was somehow comforting. He couldn't recall falling asleep, but he must have.

When had he turned off the set?

Or had he?

As Keith struggled to clear his head and piece together the tail end of his evening, the scent of coffee became stronger.

And then he realized why.

"Hi, you're up," Kenzie said as if it was an event she'd

been waiting for. She placed a large cup of coffee—black—in front of him.

His brain still hadn't fully clicked in, but he distinctly remembered Kenzie going home last night. "What are you doing here?"

"Putting coffee in front of you," she responded brightly. Kenzie knew that he wasn't really asking that, so she answered what she assumed was his actual question. "I let myself in this morning. I hope you don't mind."

The fog was still hovering around his brain, clouding it. "I gave you a key?" Keith couldn't remember doing that.

And, it turned out, with good reason.

"No," Kenzie answered. "But there was an extra front door key hanging on the key rack in the kitchen, so I took it last night. I need to get an early start this morning, and I didn't want to wake you up."

The information was going in, but it still wasn't finding a proper home. "Early start?" he echoed. "Doing what?"

"Inventory," she answered. And then she prodded his memory a little more. "You hired me to organize an estate sale, remember?"

"I know," he bit out impatiently, "but what I remember is you taking over my mother's funeral arrangements—not that I'm not glad you did," he quickly interjected, afraid that she might just back off and subsequently out of everything if she thought he was complaining. Now that apparently everyone was coming to the house after the funeral, he definitely wanted Kenzie to remain and act as his buffer.

Looking to move on, Keith picked up the mug from the coffee table. The coffee immediately drew the focus of his attention. In this day and age of designer coffee, his own taste in coffee had remained unchanged.

After taking an appreciative first sip, he raised his eyes to hers and asked, "How did you know that I take it black?"

"I guessed," Kenzie confessed. "No cream, no sugar, just black. It seemed to me that would be your style," she added.

"And strong." Which he discovered after taking his second sip of the hot brew. His first reaction hadn't been a fluke. The coffee tasted as if it could double as a paint remover.

"Another guess," she admitted. "There's also breakfast in the kitchen if you like," she added. Keith must have looked puzzled, because she elaborated. "Eggs, bacon, toast. Nothing fancy, just hot."

"I didn't see any eggs or bacon in the refrigerator."

"That's because there weren't any. I stopped at the store on my way here."

That seemed to him unnecessarily complicated. "Would've been easier stopping at a drive-through," was his assessment.

"Maybe," Kenzie conceded. "But I like to cook, and most breakfasts are simple enough to make. This certainly was," she added. "So, if you're interested, the plate's on the stove, still warm."

With that, she turned away and headed toward the stairs.

"Where are you going?" Keith asked. He got up, holding the coffee mug in both hands.

"Upstairs. Inventory," she answered again. Then she asked with a patient smile, "Remember?"

Keith frowned. He figured that he had to in order to maintain the ruse that he was effectively keeping Kenzie at arm's length, even though that length was definitely shrinking—by the moment, it seemed.

He wasn't happy about it. At the same time, he didn't seem to be able to do anything about it.

In self-defense, he allowed his temper to surface.

"Yes, I remember," he answered curtly. "I'm not senile yet."

"Yet," Kenzie echoed with a grin, clearly amused.

It was slowly working out, she thought as she hurried up the stairs. He sounded reasonably awake and somewhat cheerful—until he realized he was thawing and made a stab at grumpiness. She figured it was best to quit while she was ahead.

Besides, she had a lot of work cut out for her that had nothing to do with the state of his disposition—even though it interested her a great deal.

*Later*, she promised herself.

He'd finished eating and the dishes were in the sink, obviously waiting to be washed at some future date, whenever he felt like getting around to it.

Since Kenzie hadn't been gone all that long, he was surprised to see her.

The expression on her face was difficult for him to decipher. As a lawyer, he'd learned how to read jurists, but she was a challenge. Though she was deceptively laid-back with amusement in her eyes, he knew there was a great deal more to her than was visible at first.

"Something wrong?" Keith asked.

She wouldn't have called it "wrong" but just something that needed to be addressed. "I found a box," she began slowly, wondering how he was going to react.

"So?" he asked, waiting for some sort of further explanation.

"It's a box of letters," Kenzie told him, sounding slightly

breathless as she placed the box on the coffee table in front of him.

Keith shrugged. He refrained from touching it, as if not touching the box allowed him to negate the validity of whatever might have been inside. He regarded it uneasily without knowing why.

"Put it in the trash," he told her. "Nobody's going to want to read someone else's letters."

"The letters are ones your mother wrote to you," she told him quietly.

Keith looked at her sharply. There was an angry accusation in his eyes.

What sort of game was she playing? "I never got any letters from her," he informed Kenzie coldly.

"They weren't mailed." She glanced down at the box. "They were addressed, stamped, signed, but she never mailed them."

He felt a ripple of curiosity forming—and smashed it. "I told you, put them in the trash."

She stared at him as if he'd just instructed her to set the house on fire. "Don't you want to read what she wanted to tell you?"

"If my mother *wanted* to tell me anything, she would have mailed the letters," he said coldly. "Consequently, what she wrote there was for her own conscience. It had nothing to do with me."

She didn't believe that—and neither did Keith, she thought. "But—"

Keith cut her short. "Look, I know you think you're helping, but you're not," he said forcefully. "You've already done more than you're supposed to, and no matter what misguided notion you might have, it's not your job to be my conscience. Either stop, or I'll pay you for the time you've put in so far, and I'll get someone else to handle this so-called estate sale."

She suppressed a sigh, picking up the box again. "You're going to regret not reading these."

"My letters, my regret."

Kenzie looked down at the box she'd picked up, then moved it against the crook of her arm. "Have it your way."

*Finally!*

"Thank you," Keith said. The words were polite and perfunctory. He'd honestly expected more of an argument out of her than that.

Kenzie merely nodded her acknowledgment as she walked out of the kitchen, carrying the offending box of letters out with her. She cradled the box against her as if she were carrying a baby.

She disappeared from view, and Keith turned back around again, fairly certain that the incident was closed. Nonetheless, he strained to hear the familiar sounds of Kenzie going out of the house so that she could throw the letters away.

And then he did.

He heard the front door open and then close again. He sat, waiting to hear it open again. When it didn't, he began to wonder if Kenzie had opted to take him up on the alternative that he offered and decided to leave.

He remained at the table, straining to hear some movement from the front of the house.

When he finally heard the door opening again, he released the breath he'd unconsciously been holding.

She hadn't left.

The relief he felt surprised him.

And worried him, as well.

## Chapter Seven

Keith had no time to examine his rather strong—and positive—reaction to the fact that Kenzie hadn't left. The moment she walked back into the room, she hit him with a question.

"Are you planning on going to the funeral home today?"

He thought it was rather an odd question, coming from her. After all, her actual function here was to organize what was in the house, put a price on it and, hopefully, sell it. Granted, she was being helpful in other ways, but she *had* volunteered her services. He hadn't recruited her. In no way was that even remotely associated with his attendance—or nonattendance—at the funeral home.

"No," he responded. "Why would you want to know that?"

She shrugged carelessly and said, "No reason. I just thought you might want to be there to talk to some of her friends in case they had any questions or just wanted to talk to you."

"I'll be at the funeral," he reminded her somewhat stiffly. "If they have anything to ask, they can do it then." Although the very thought of being subjected to any sort of questions regarding his mother's final days—or even her final years—left him feeling exceedingly uncomfortable. He wouldn't be able to answer any of them because, quite frankly, he didn't know anything about the last ten years. His mother's supposed letters to him notwithstanding, there had been no contact between them during that time.

"Or they can ask you at the reception," she reminded him.

For a second, he'd forgotten about the reception. More to endure, he thought wearily. He didn't even bother attempting to contain the less than happy sigh that escaped. "Yeah, there's that, too."

She squashed the desire to offer him any comfort. The Keith standing before her wasn't the type to accept any overt gestures. That was why she had to go the indirect route she was taking.

"Well, if you're not going to the funeral home, why don't you come with me?"

"Come with you where?" he asked suspiciously.

Instead of answering his question, Kenzie hit him with a question of her own. "You don't like surprises, do you?"

"Surprises don't usually turn out to be a good thing."

She thought of the family gathering she was trying to bring him to. A fondness slipped over her, the way it always did whenever she thought of her family en masse. "Well, in this case I can guarantee you good food, good spirits and maybe even some singing." He still appeared rather skeptical about the whole idea—and she could tell that the singing part was definitely *not* a selling feature.

Still, she tried to make him come around by promising, "It'll be good for you."

The frown on Keith's face deepened. "The last time I heard that line, I was facing a plate of steamed vegetables."

Kenzie suppressed a laugh. "I promise this experience will be way better than a plate of vegetables. And it'll help you unwind."

That only managed to put him on his guard. "What makes you think I need to unwind?"

Kenzie rolled her eyes in response to his question. She couldn't help it. "Oh, please. I've seen balls of yarn that were less wound up than you."

Passing by him at the table, she crossed over to the sink. Kenzie turned on the water and began washing the dishes.

Still nursing the last of his coffee, Keith half rose in his seat. "You don't have to do that," he protested.

Maybe not, but someone had to, and she'd learned that molehills were a lot easier to tackle than mountains.

"Mrs. Sommers'll be showing the house soon. You don't want to let things like dirty dishes start accumulating."

She was doing it again, acting as if she knew him better than he knew himself. "What makes you think I wasn't going to wash those?" he asked.

Kenzie stopped washing for a minute and looked at him over her shoulder. Her answer to that was simplicity itself. "You're a man."

Keith scowled. "What's that supposed to mean?"

The smile on her lips softened the sting. "There are certain edicts out there in the cosmos. One of them states that men don't do dishes. They buy dishes, break dishes, sometimes borrow dishes, but they don't wash them if they can avoid it at all."

"Doesn't that smack of sexism?" he asked, prodding her.

"Maybe," Kenzie allowed generously. "That still doesn't change the fact that it's true," she concluded with a smile, then got back to her initial topic. "So, since you're not going to the funeral home, two o'clock okay with you?"

He was still distrustful of where this was going. Being a lawyer had changed the way he looked at everything. "For what?"

"For me to pick you up so you can come with me," she told him innocently, then asked, "Are you always this inattentive?"

"Only when I'm not interested," Keith replied truthfully.

"This'll do you good," she promised.

"You keep saying that. Just what sort of good would going off with you do me?" he asked.

Was she coming on to him? he suddenly wondered. He wouldn't have thought so. He had to admit that the idea was definitely not without its appeal. The woman was extremely compelling and, under other circumstances, he could see himself being really attracted to her—and acting on it. But he wasn't going to stay here long enough to even entertain that possibility, much less explore it. And he had never been into one-night stands.

"That's where the surprise part of this comes in," she told him glibly, coming full circle.

He fixed her with a look. "I think we've had this dance before."

Kenzie merely smiled, unfazed by the fact that he was leveling an accusation at her. "We have," she acknowledged, then proposed, "This time, just for fun, why don't you let me lead?"

What did he have to lose? Keith asked himself gamely. After all, in just three days, four at the most, he wasn't even going to be in the same longitude and latitude as this woman or as anyone else around here, for that matter.

Besides, he had to admit he did like her company—for the most part.

"Okay, why not?" he said with a shrug, surrendering—for now.

"Great," she answered. This had actually turned out to be easier than she thought.

Enthused—and because she did know him and they did go back all the way to high school—Kenzie allowed herself to go with her impulse. It was her way, but not usually with someone as standoffish as Keith had become.

Turning from the sink, her hands still wet from the dishes she'd just finished washing, Kenzie threw her arms around his neck and kissed him.

Her aim—and intention—had been to kiss his cheek. But, surprised by her sudden movement, he'd turned his head at the last second to look at her, puzzled.

He was about to ask her what she was doing, which was how his mouth happened to be open when her lips missed their intended target and instead locked onto his.

To say that he was surprised would have been a huge understatement.

In actuality, they were *both* surprised.

And even more surprising than that was the realization that something was going on here that went beyond the simple contact of lips. Way beyond.

This was the fantasy that she had nurtured the two years they had both been in high school at the same time.

Night after night, she'd dreamed about what it might actually feel like, kissing Keith. *Being* kissed by Keith.

Dreams, she now realized, didn't begin to do the actual sensation justice, even though this kiss had been unintentional.

Kenzie felt as if she had swallowed a match. A *lit* match, and it was setting her on fire. But it was a very pleasant, enjoyable fire, and with very little effort—

*No, hold it*, the voice of common sense all but screamed in her head in an attempt to redirect her attention. This just couldn't happen. At least, not by accident. If it did, that almost made her a predator. Whether he would admit it or not—whether he even *knew* it or not—Keith was very vulnerable right now, and she was taking advantage of that as surely as if she was a stalker, jumping at the first glimmer of an opportunity.

It didn't matter that she was as caught by surprise as he was. That she hadn't meant to do anything more than kiss his cheek. Circumstances had abruptly changed, and she needed to take that into account and backpedal as quickly as she could before something happened that couldn't be undone.

*In a second*, something inside her promised breathlessly, stalling for time.

He'd told Kenzie the truth. He didn't like surprises. But this—this was different. While it still fell under the general heading of being a surprise, it was so much more. He had no idea where to begin to categorize it or file it away. He clearly hadn't meant for this to happen, but now that it had, he was forced to look at Kenzie in a whole different light.

This was the girl he had gone to school with? The one everyone had laughingly referred to as Clumsy Mac?

Talk about still waters running deep. There was an entire sea here.

When contact between them was abruptly severed—and she had been the one to sever it, just as she had been the one to initiate it—Keith saw her flush and then mumble something that sounded like "Oops."

The word echoed back in his head, as if he'd somehow hit instant replay. The whole scenario struck him as ludicrous.

Before he could stop himself, he started to laugh.

Laugh so hard that his sides actually shook. And then tears came to his eyes. Whether they'd initially been stored there against anticipated further sorrow, he didn't know.

The laughter and the accompanying tears didn't abate immediately, not until he was almost exhausted.

Kenzie joined in and couldn't seem to stop, either, not until they both collapsed onto the floor in a crumbled heap, both too exhausted to move.

Finally, drawing in deep breaths, Keith found that his sanity was slowly restored.

"What just happened here?" he was finally able to ask, still bemused.

"I'm not sure," Kenzie told him honestly as she gathered herself together. "But I think we both needed it."

Though he wanted to protest, he knew she was right. He didn't exactly feel rejuvenated, but the oppressiveness that had been weighing him down the last few days seemed to have taken a few steps back, allowing him to regain his sense of self.

"So now what?" Keith asked, curious as to what she would say.

"Now we each take care of a few minor things that we need to see to, and I'll be back by two to pick you up."

Keith took in a deep breath. He was already having second thoughts that he'd said yes too soon and that he was going to regret this.

"About that—" he began.

Kenzie immediately began to shake her head, as if his words wouldn't be able to gain access to a moving target. "Sorry," she said, cutting Keith off before he could get any further. "My hearing seems to be clogged. Must have happened during that laugh-fest we just shared. Gotta run," she announced quickly, deliberately talking too fast for him to be able to get in a word edgewise.

Keith opened and then closed his mouth one last time as he heard the front door close with finality. He felt a little as if he'd been blitzkrieged.

The odd thing was, he discovered he wasn't angry or even mildly annoyed about it.

Instead, his mouth was curving in just the vaguest hint of a smile.

Kenzie wasn't true to her word. She wasn't back by two.

She was back *before* two.

MacKenzie Bradshaw was the only woman he'd ever encountered who was early, Keith thought with grudging admiration.

Though he had a feeling it was futile, he attempted to beg off one last time. "Look, I know I kind of agreed before, but—"

Kenzie flashed the same innocent look in response. "Still have that hearing problem," she told him. "Maybe it'll clear up by the time we get there."

It was a game and she knew it. A game because if Keith really didn't want to go, there was no way she could actually *make* him go. So these were just motions he was going through, possibly to satisfy some inner need to tell himself that he'd tried to resist but had gone along with what she proposed for reasons of maintaining the peace.

"Exactly where is 'there'?" she heard Keith asking her even as he followed her out of the house.

"The place we're supposed to be," she answered evasively, waiting for him to lock the front door.

Keith pocketed his key. For some odd reason, this effervescent woman had stirred his curiosity. He pretended to resist for form's sake, and he knew that she was aware of it. There was no question that if he really didn't want to do something or go somewhere, he didn't. It was that simple. He wasn't exactly a ninety-eight-pound weakling who could be flung over an adversary's shoulder and carried off, fireman style. At six-two, Keith couldn't be carried off anywhere.

But he wanted to see exactly where Kenzie felt he needed to go, so he went along with this, telling himself at he could bail at any time, calling a halt to it and just going home.

He noted that Kenzie, who was always dressed attractively, hadn't done anything out of the ordinary to her appearance, so they weren't going anywhere that required formal wear.

Apparently that was the only clue she was dispensing, because when he asked for more information, Kenzie very deftly sidestepped and avoided his attempts to extract it from her.

"And if I just refuse to go?" he asked as he watched her slide behind the steering wheel of her car.

"You promised me a filet mignon dinner if I deciphered your mother's handwriting in her address book, remember?"

He remembered. When he'd made the bet, he'd done

it knowing that if she won, it would allow him to take her out without the formality of actually *asking* her out. "We're going to dinner?" he questioned.

"No, but this can be in place of that." Kenzie put it in simpler terms. "You come with me, I absolve you of that bet. Fair enough?"

"Fair?" he echoed. In all honesty, he couldn't really answer that without getting further information to work with. Information he already knew he wasn't about to get ahead of time. She'd made that abundantly clear. "Ask me again after I get back," he told her.

A smile that could be described as nothing short of sexy, even by the most oblivious of people, curved the corners of her mouth.

At first glance, Keith found his reaction to the sight of her smile rather unsettling. And yet at the same time, the sight of her smile directed at him was oddly appealing.

At the root of it all, he had to surmise, was the accidental kiss they'd shared this morning. It had placed an entirely different spin on just about everything going on between them.

It certainly affected how he looked at her.

Maybe it had something to do with where he found himself right now—at loose ends, maybe even cast adrift. In two days he would have to go through the motions of a pantomime he had no desire to endure.

At this funeral, the attendees would be expecting him to play the part of a grieving son, but he'd been that already. Ten years ago he'd been that grieving son, as well as a grieving brother.

To lose Amy had been extremely rough on his soul. To lose his mother in the bargain had been all but crushing for him. He hadn't lost his mother literally—she was, after all, still breathing—but for all intents and purposes, he had lost the mother he had known all his life up to that tragic point.

After Amy died in the accident, his kind, loving, levelheaded mother had suddenly transformed into what amounted to a reckless teenager. As far as he was concerned, there was nothing more pitiable than a fifty-year-old teenager, but she had refused to listen to anything he said. He tried to reason with her, even asked her to seek help, but she'd turned him down. Desperate, hurting, he had continued to cajole and plead until finally he'd lost all patience with her.

And then one day, the collision he knew was coming came. Heated, angry words were exchanged. Words that, once they were out, couldn't be taken back.

Words that destroyed all the bridges that connected them to each other.

And even if those words could be taken back, they certainly couldn't be erased from memory. That was where they remained forever, and because they were there, nothing else was allowed to thrive.

"Are you all right?" Kenzie asked him gently.

Snapping out of it, Keith looked at her. "Yeah, sure. Why?"

"You got really quiet there, and you've got this strange look on your face," she told him.

Keith forced himself to smile for a second, pretending he hadn't been preoccupied with any sort of serious thoughts. "Just contemplating what kind of torture you have in mind for me."

Kenzie wasn't sure she believed him, but she played along, anyway. There was no point in pressing him. "Not torture," she promised. "And you'll see soon enough."

"I suppose I will," he replied quietly.

He didn't fool her for a minute, but the game continued, anyway. She was counting on her family to help her bring him around to the person she knew he used to be.

## Chapter Eight

"It's a house," he said in surprise as Kenzie began to slow down at the curb before the well-kept two-story structure.

They'd turned in to a residential development, so he shouldn't have been surprised, but for some reason he'd thought she might be taking him to a more public place.

There was amusement in Kenzie's eyes as she smiled at him. "Nothing wrong with your powers of observation, I see."

He had no idea if she was being sarcastic or not. Had the words come from anyone else, he would have gone with the former. But from what he remembered of her from high school and what he'd been exposed to currently, Kenzie was far too positive a person to waste her time with sarcasm.

"It's my mom's house," she told Keith as she brought her vehicle to a complete stop and turned off the engine. Kenzie could see that he was less than thrilled about being exposed to family, even if that family belonged to some-one else. "Ginny's having a birthday party."

He left his seat belt buckled even though she was undo-ing hers. He had no idea who Kenzie was talking about. "Ginny?" he questioned.

Kenzie nodded, wondering if he was going to give her a hard time, after all. "One of my nieces. She's three today."

"You brought me to a kid's birthday party?" he asked in disbelief. This was what he got for letting his guard down and going along.

"I brought you to a *family* birthday party," Kenzie cor-rected him. "It just happens to be Ginny's birthday. If this had been two weeks ago, it would have been my mother's birthday. Most of the family live pretty busy lives," she went on, opening the door on her side. "Birthdays are the excuse we use to get together for a few hours."

He wasn't moving. Pausing, she bent down and looked into the car at him. "The car's too big to fit in the living room," she said matter-of-factly.

His eyebrows drew together. "What?"

"You're still buckled up," Kenzie said, nodding at the fastened seat belt. "And I just thought you'd want to know that the car is too big to take in with you, so you're going to have to unbuckle the seat belt."

He was clearly having his doubts about attending. "Maybe I should just stay here until you're done."

"Maybe you shouldn't," Kenzie countered cheerfully. "The whole point is to get you out of the house and clear your head," she told him.

He had his own way of unwinding that didn't involve pretending to be interested in what strangers were talk-ing about. "A glass of wine will clear my head."

"Not hardly," she told him. "Wine just makes things

fuzzy. C'mon," she coaxed him. "I've got a very friendly family and they don't bite—I promise. Besides, if you come in with me, you'll be doing me a favor."

"What kind of a favor?" Keith asked suspiciously. His hand hovered over the seat belt, which remained buckled.

She thought back to the other day and her sister's attempts to set her up with a blind date for dinner at her house. "If my siblings see me coming in with a breathing male under the age of fifty, they might leave me alone for a while."

He was no more enlightened now than he had been a moment ago. "I don't get it."

Sighing, Kenzie spelled it out for him. "They're all married. I'm not. I'm the youngest and somehow, through no fault of my own, I became everyone's favorite matchmaking project. If they see you, they'll cease and desist— at least for a little while—and I can breathe and focus on doing my job well instead of having to fend off their efforts."

Now he understood. "That sounds reasonable enough, I guess."

"Great." She closed the door on her side. "Now take a deep breath," she advised. "And let's go."

The second Keith got out of her car, Kenzie aimed her key fob at the vehicle and pressed it. Four locks all closed simultaneously.

The sounds of people talking, laughing, calling out to one another were all around him long before the front door of the house was opened.

Echoes from long ago rose up to meet Keith, and he stopped short of the front step.

He didn't know if he was up to this, willingly walking into a situation that was already resurrecting memories he had absolutely no desire to revisit.

Memories that had been, until now, too painful for him.

The next moment, just before he started to turn away, he felt Kenzie weaving her arm through his as if it were a long practiced maneuver. Before he could say a word in protest—or tell her that he had definitely changed his mind—the front door opened, and he found himself drawn inside by a woman with warm eyes and a warmer smile. A woman, he realized, who looked exactly like an older version of Kenzie.

"Come in. You're just in time," she told them.

"Just in time?" he repeated more quietly, glancing at Kenzie as they followed the woman into the living room—a room filled with people, large and small.

"She means that they haven't sung 'Happy Birthday' yet. Mom," Kenzie said, raising her voice as she called out to the older woman. When Mrs. Bradshaw turned around, Kenzie said, "You remember Keith O'Connell. Keith, this is my mom, Andrea."

"Yes, of course," Andrea replied, taking his hand and shaking it.

He didn't see how that was possible—he had no memory of ever encountering the woman—but he played along and returned the smile.

Keith still didn't want to be here, but he couldn't leave without causing a scene. That seemed like rather a ludicrous thing to do, given that the people here were participating in a child's birthday party, so he refrained.

Making the best of it, Keith told himself that for the duration of an hour or ninety minutes, he could put up with this charade. For some reason, Kenzie wanted him here, and in a way, he did owe her. After all, she had handled all the extraneous details surrounding the funeral and reception for him. And that, in turn, had taken some of the weight of this whole experience off his shoulders.

"Kenzie, you made it. And you brought a man." The woman who swooped down on them from the left looked as if she were another older version of Kenzie. Younger than her mother, so this had to be a sister, he guessed. An older, *pregnant* sister, he amended as he got a better view of the woman who was currently giving him a very thorough once-over.

"Yes, I did, but he's not for Ginny," Kenzie responded, smiling at her sister. "This," she continued, placing the gaily wrapped package she had brought with her into her sister's hands, "is for our birthday girl."

"And this is?" Marcy asked, clearly not easily diverted. She also didn't bother to hide the fact that she was still giving her sister's companion a very close inspection.

After another moment, Kenzie gathered from the expression on Marcy's face that Keith had met with her sister's guarded approval.

"Is Keith," Kenzie answered, deliberately being mysterious and leaving out his last name. "That's all you need to know. Keith, meet Marcy Bradshaw Crawford. She's just one of my meddlesome siblings," she warned him. "All four of them smile and look harmless, but trust me, they're not. This, however," Kenzie declared, never missing a beat as she scooped up her niece, who had launched herself at her from across the room, "is a regular little charmer. However, she's prone to sneak attacks."

Laughing, she swung the little girl around in a circle before putting Ginny down again. "Don't turn your back on her for a second," she told Keith.

She said it so seriously that Ginny looked up at her, an impatient expression on her small, thin face. "Don't worry. I won't hurt him, Aunt Kenzie."

"I know, Pumpkin. But you're quick, and I'm afraid that my friend here isn't used to that." She'd said that strictly for Ginny's benefit, so the little girl would feel more confident about herself. An anticipated new arrival in the family was a time for shifting dynamics and self-doubts, and she just wanted to be sure that her niece was equipped to weather it well.

Kenzie tousled the little girl's hair, knowing the day wasn't far away that Ginny would be looking to disentangle herself from her parents and the rest of the family and go off with her friends.

*Way of the world*, she thought with resignation.

Keith had assumed that he could just remain on the sidelines, hidden in plain sight, so to speak. That way, he didn't have to get involved in any of the conversations that were going on all around him.

Or so he thought, only to discover he was sadly mistaken.

There was no such thing as standing on the sidelines when it came to Kenzie's family. He found himself engulfed in warm voices, had questions directed at him that rang with genuine interest and was on the receiving end of amusing stories to the extent that he quickly discovered he didn't even know which way to turn or whose question to answer first.

He also discovered that there was no place to hide. Even more surprising, he didn't really want to, at least not all that much.

To his relief, Kenzie came to his rescue when he found himself facing questions about the cases he took on as a lawyer.

"No shop talk, Tom," she told her brother, wedging herself in between her oldest sibling and Keith. "I promised Keith that this afternoon was all about unwinding, not grilling."

Slipping her arm through his, she gently led Keith away from the small cluster of guests.

"I take it we're not leaving yet," Keith said. To his own surprise, he wasn't having that bad a time. This experience, forced though it was, was not without its merits.

"Soon," she murmured, drawing him over to another gathering.

She repeatedly came to his rescue several more times that afternoon and early evening.

Contrary to what he thought was happening—that he would stay for a total of sixty minutes, maybe ninety— by the end of his self-imposed time limit, Keith discovered that he was more than amenable to remaining for a little while longer.

That officially ended as dusk was creeping up out of the Pacific waters, looking to embrace whatever it could in order to remain around.

At first, Keith had really tried not to take part in the conversations. He thought, after remaining deliberately closed-mouthed once or twice, that would be the end of it.

However, he had no idea just how unobtrusively persistent Kenzie's family members—from the oldest member to the youngest—could be when it came to doing something they believed, in their heart of hearts, was the right thing. Apparently, getting him to talk fell under that heading.

Drawing him out in conversation had been tricky to say the least, but to Keith's amazement, he was no match for even the youngest of Kenzie's clan.

And just like that, he was pulled in.

Pulled into the conversation and consequently, by and by, pulled into the family dynamic, as well.

That was how one hour turned into two and two into

four. Before he knew it, most of the day had gone by. Moreover, he wasn't the least bit annoyed by this.

He liked these unassuming, down-to-earth people even though he initially felt that he had nothing in common with them. But he—and they—had all initially come from a working class mother and father who took on any kind of work to keep their children dressed and fed. That, he discovered, was the American dream to Kenzie's parents, and they had captured it in the palms of their hands, passing it down to their children.

And although it was very much against his will at first, when Kenzie's mother came up to him to exchange a few words later that evening, Keith couldn't help thinking of his own mother—the way she had once been, not the woman whose burial service he was going to be attending the day after tomorrow.

With a great deal of effort, Keith shook off the memory. Nothing good would come of going there. He had to remember that—and resist the temptation to do otherwise.

"I think our birthday girl is ready to be taken home, don't you?" Andrea asked him.

The little girl was sitting beside him on the sofa, her head lolling to one side. She was obviously asleep and had been for the last twenty minutes or so, after valiantly struggling to keep her eyes open. She'd finally lost the battle. Her even, measured breathing attested to that.

"It is getting late," Keith agreed. His mother had been very strict about bedtime when he was Ginny's age. Apparently, Kenzie's family didn't feel the same way.

Kenzie picked up his cue. Looking at Keith, she inclined her head so that only he could hear her and said, "You've more than paid off your debt. Would you like to go back to your house?"

The candles had been blown out and the cake had long

since been eaten. Ginny had gone on to daintily remove the wrapping paper from her gifts. Some of the paper, evading cleanup, still littered parts of the floor. Ginny might have fallen asleep, but her older cousins were awake, and some of them were playing with her gifts, all under their mothers' watchful eyes.

All in all, it was a scene out of a Norman Rockwell painting, only done one better. Keith felt a very odd sensation of longing stirring inside before he managed to block it and lock it away.

"Are you serious?" Keith asked, surprised that Kenzie would come around so easily—and on her own, too. He had become fairly convinced that in order to leave the premises before midnight, he would be forced to come up with some sort of an elaborate escape plan.

Not that he really wanted to all that much.

Maybe there was something in the punch, Keith thought.

Obviously amused by his response, Kenzie grinned at him. That grin was getting to him, working its way under his skin. He was finding her harder and harder to ignore or even keep at bay.

"It would be too cruel to tease you like that," she told him, whispering the words into his ear and creating, unbeknownst to her, waves of warmth that undulated through him. "Yes, I'm serious," she assured him.

To prove it, Kenzie rose to her feet.

The birthday girl chose that moment to wake up. Rubbing her eyes, Ginny looked up at her aunt. The expression on her face silently asked if the fact that Kenzie was on her feet meant that another present was possibly coming her way.

"We've got to get going, sweetie," she told Ginny— and thereby also informed all those who needed to be informed that they were leaving. "We've got a lot of things to do tomorrow."

Rather than say anything to her, Ginny turned to look at Keith. With all the guile of a four-year-old, she asked, "Are you gonna come back?"

The little girl had caught him completely off guard. When Keith opened his mouth, it was to offer what he felt was a valid excuse. "I don't live around here."

"But you can always come back," Ginny pointed out.

"Maybe some time," Keith conceded evasively, not about to get into involved explanations. It occurred to him that he couldn't remember the last time someone had actually *wanted* his presence enough to question the excuse he offered.

"He's going to be very busy, Ginny," Kenzie said, once again coming to his rescue.

"But sometime?" she questioned hopefully, looking at Keith with large, soulful blue eyes.

"Sometime," Kenzie echoed, making the nebulous word sound more like a promise.

Ginny flashed Kenzie a big smile, then surprised Keith by jumping to her feet and awarding him a quick, fierce hug before turning her attention back to her newly acquired loot.

"You look stunned," Kenzie observed as they made their way to the door amid a chorus of goodbyes from the people who remained. "Never been hugged by a little girl before?" she guessed.

He thought of making some sort of flippant remark or excuse, then reconsidered and went with the plain truth. "Not to my recollection."

"Makes you feel good, doesn't it?"

He grunted something unintelligible. It was enough to make her smile to herself.

"I think you made a big impression on my niece," Kenzie said as they were walking back to her car. "As well as on my family," she added.

To her surprise, Keith had actually remembered most of her family's names during the course of the day. That nice guy she'd been trying to reach was beginning to surface.

The moon lit their way, allowing her to see Keith's expression. It had been a long day, and part of her had expected him to be annoyed or, at the very least, beleaguered. But he appeared to be neither. That was another nice surprise.

"Yeah, well, that worked both ways," Keith told her after a couple of beats.

Kenzie got the impression that he had first debated the pros and cons of voicing his reaction to the little girl before saying anything.

"You have a nice family."

He couldn't have said anything better or more meaningful to her.

"Thanks. I think so," she said without any hesitation or embarrassment. "There are times I'd like to strangle one or more of my siblings, but for the most part, I have to agree with you. They really *are* nice." Then she added, "I'll bet you're really tired. I'd better take you home so you get enough rest to help me tackle the pricing tomorrow."

"Pricing?" he echoed, confused.

"Of the things going into the first wave of the estate sale. I decided that it should start tomorrow." That had changed from her original plan, but she thought it best to keep Keith busy rather than dwelling on the situation—and his loss, even if he didn't want to admit it. "Remember? I asked if you had any objections to doing it before the funeral, and you were all for getting started."

He grunted in agreement, but the truth of it was, he'd actually forgotten that conversation. Attending the birthday party, being transported down memory lane by a family-friendly scenario that was so similar to what he'd grown up with, had temporarily driven thoughts of everything else out of his head.

But it all came back to him now as reality returned to wrap him in its cold embrace.

He pushed the emotion aside and dwelled only on what needed to be done.

## Chapter Nine

He'd meant to be gone before the whole thing got underway.

When he had fallen asleep last night, Keith had had every intention of being gone before the estate sale, or even the preparations for displaying the items, had begun. Although if he were being honest with himself, he hadn't really a clue as to where "gone" was physically located. He hadn't gotten that far along in figuring out his escape plan when sleep had suddenly—and silently—overtaken him.

Sleep had brought dreams, something that he hadn't experienced in a very long time. Years, as a matter of fact. Nocturnal episodes in his life these past few years were defined by being awake, then finding himself waking up. Sleep, obviously, occurred in between those two end posts, but it brought no dreams with it that he was aware of, certainly none that he could summon once his eyes were open and his brain shook off its fuzzy, unfocused state.

But last night had been different. Last night, when he'd fallen asleep, he'd had dreams, tiny snatches of dreams. Dreams that couldn't have lasted for more than a few moments. Dreams that he was in this house, the house where he'd grown up, but rather than Amy and his mother, the people inhabiting his childhood home had been Kenzie's family.

A couple of times during these disjointed, rambling segments that seemed to fill his head, he thought he'd caught sight of Amy. When that happened, he immediately attempted to follow her. But whenever he entered the room he was positive she was in, he found he was wrong. She wasn't there. In her place were a whole bunch of nieces and nephews and various assorted other relatives, all of whom belonged to Kenzie.

And yet, somehow, there was this unspoken feeling that these relatives infiltrating his dreams also belonged to him.

Part of him was convinced, during these recurring sequences, that he was in fact dreaming, and all he needed to do to end this was to wake up.

Easier thought than executed.

No matter how hard he tried, his eyes just would not open, and as long as they stayed closed, he remained within the confines of this endless dreamlike state.

After numerous attempts, when Keith finally *did* manage to pry open his eyes—his lids felt as if they weighed a ton—daylight wasn't tiptoeing into the bedroom.

It had come *stomping* into the room.

The moment his brain registered that fact—as well as the fact that it was the morning of the sale—he sat bolt upright.

The sudden movement brought a severe penalty with it. His head began to pound, producing one of those inexplicable morning headaches that insisted on haunting him every so often. He'd suffered through them on occasion ever since he'd been a child. They made thinking clearly nothing short of a challenge.

Keith sat perfectly still for approximately thirty seconds, taking in a deep breath and vainly trying to center himself. When that failed, he threw off his bedclothes and went directly into his bathroom. After shedding his clothing, Keith got into the shower stall. With quick, efficient movements, he did his best to wash the imagery out of his brain as he showered.

Seven minutes later, he'd dried off, dressed and was walking out of his bedroom. In his conservative estimation, he had about fifteen minutes to vacate the premises before Kenzie arrived and descended on him.

He estimated wrong.

The second he was in the hallway, walking toward the stairs, Keith instantly knew he had sorely miscalculated. The warm, inviting aroma of coffee was wafting up the stairs and tantalized him.

It also mocked him.

He knew he hadn't had the presence of mind to program his coffeemaker last night. That meant either he had a warm, hospitable burglar who had broken into his house and decided to make coffee for him while he was at it—or Kenzie was here early, champing at the bit to get the sale underway.

Making coffee was more her style.

Keith caught part of himself rooting for the burglar. At least then he could quickly leave the premises without having to offer any excuses or to beg off.

Reminding himself that he was the one in charge here

and that Kenzie, in point of fact, actually worked for him did absolutely no good.

It wasn't that he felt he couldn't stand up to her and make his point known. It was just that for some reason, while he was standing up and making his point, Kenzie seemed able to steamroller right over logic—and him.

He ran into her on the stairs.

Kenzie was going up holding a steaming cup of hot coffee in her hands—her bribe of choice—and he was on his way down, still vainly hoping to execute some sort of an eleventh-hour great escape before she saw him. That boat, of course, had instantly sailed off the moment that their eyes met.

Kenzie grinned as she stopped walking. "You're up," she noted cheerfully.

"Looks that way," he responded, silently berating himself for not setting an alarm to wake him up earlier.

Keith glanced over her shoulder at the front door. He was just several yards short of an escape, he couldn't help thinking almost wistfully.

So near and yet so far.

"I brought you coffee," Kenzie told him.

His attention was drawn back to the woman directly in front of him. "I figured that part out on my own," he responded flippantly.

Kenzie wasn't about to comment on his less than sunny disposition. Kenzie thought his surliness might have something to do with the fact that people would be going through, paying for and carting off bits and pieces of his former life.

That had to be rough. But that was exactly why she *had* given him the option of holding some things back, of vetoing any item from going on sale.

However, he had declined to even entertain the idea,

much less executing it, saying, "As far as I'm concerned, you can sell the whole household as one big lot if it means getting rid of everything."

In her heart, she refused to believe he actually meant that. At least, she was sure he didn't mean it about *everything* in the house. The man whom she'd gotten to interact with her family was definitely not devoid of all feelings and emotions.

Those emotions and feelings were most likely buried rather deeply because of his sister's death.

People reacted differently to tragedies of that magnitude. Some rallied, and it became their finest hour. Others fell to pieces and were never quite the same again.

Most people, however, fell somewhere in between, with an entire spectrum of emotions. And she wanted to help him navigate the spectrum if she possibly could.

Surrendering the coffee cup to him, Kenzie made a U-turn on the stairs and headed back down. "There's breakfast in the kitchen if you're interested," she added.

"Good place for it,"

Hand on the banister, Kenzie paused and looked over her shoulder at him. "*Your* breakfast."

He did his best to seem disinterested, fully aware now that if he gave Kenzie an inch, she would create a little village on it.

"I didn't ask for any."

The coffee felt like liquid heaven going down, though. He was forced to admit secretly that the woman really knew how to make one hell of a cup of coffee.

"No, you didn't," Kenzie agreed. "But you do need to eat and keep up your strength."

He stared at the back of the blond head as he walked behind her. That was an odd thing to say, he thought. Why would she think he needed strength? "Are you entering me in a weight lifting contest?"

Coming to the bottom of the stairs, she turned around to look at him. "No, but I would like you to carry some things out to the driveway for me. Pablo pulled a muscle, so I told him to stay home and take care of himself."

"Pablo?" he echoed. Who was that? He was fairly certain he hadn't met anyone by that name at her niece's birthday party last night.

"Pablo's my assistant and general, all-around handy person," she explained.

"I take it he's not very handy with a pulled muscle." Finishing off the coffee, Keith left the cup on the first flat surface nearest the staircase.

"None of us is." Deftly she scooped up the cup, quickly carrying it to the kitchen, where his breakfast was waiting for him beneath a covered dish on the kitchen counter. "And, like I said, he's home, resting. I arranged everything that's going on sale today in boxes, but now the boxes need to find their way outside to the tables."

"Tables?"

Nothing was making immediate sense to him. Keith was beginning to feel like Alice in Wonderland after she slid down the rabbit hole. Quite an identity crisis for a thirty-two-year-old male, he couldn't help thinking.

Kenzie nodded, patiently explaining, "The ones I set up under the canopy in your driveway."

"My driveway—the driveway," he amended, still doing his best to distance himself from the house and the woman who had lived alone here for the past ten years, "doesn't have a canopy."

"It does for today," she contradicted him. "And for later this week when the sales resume."

Because she wanted to be respectful of his mother, she

was putting the sale on hold the day of the funeral. But since Keith was in a hurry to have it all over with, the sale would resume the day after that.

"The canopy catches the neighbors' eye—and it also protects some of the more delicate items from being damaged by the sun," she added. "Don't forget, some of the things are old and very delicate."

Keith just shook his head. She had gone too far in her efforts to protect things he had no use for or desire to preserve.

"You're the expert," he commented in a tone that said what he thought was the exact opposite.

Kenzie took pride in the fact that she was good at her job and even better at not getting drawn into any sort of a confrontation about minor matters. Long ago, she had learned to pick her fights, and this was definitely not meant to be one of them. She sensed that despite Keith's bravado, he *was* having a hard time with what was happening.

For all she knew, he hadn't even made his peace with his mother's death. If that was the case, it would hit him really hard down the line.

"Thank you for that," she said quietly. "Now eat your breakfast while it's still warm and then come out and help me show off the first wave of items to their best advantage."

Keith picked up the dish from the counter, removing the cover and leaving it behind. He sat down at the table. He noticed she'd set utensils out for him. She didn't miss a thing.

"It's a glorified garage sale," he pointed out. "There *is* no showing things off to their best advantage, no matter what you try."

Kenzie was not easily dissuaded. Flashing one of her

dazzling smiles, she told him as she left the kitchen, "You'd be surprised."

And, he discovered shortly thereafter, he was.

Half an hour after he had carried out close to ten boxes of memorabilia and then retreated into the house, Keith moved the curtain aside from the living room window and saw that there were people lining up on his driveway, waiting their turn to approach the very end of a long table.

They were holding items they had discovered at the sale in one hand and money in the other. They were all queuing up to reach Kenzie. She was on the other side of the long rectangular table, ringing up these found treasures on what looked to be an old-fashioned cash register.

Keith decided that it was time for him to make himself scarce.

He had no attachment to these items, he silently insisted for the tenth or so time. But watching them being snatched up and then paraded out to waiting vehicles still felt somewhat disconcerting to him.

Rather than attempt to explore the reason he'd feel this way, Keith decided not to witness any of it.

Grabbing a jacket—December in Southern California didn't exactly bring visions of icicles to mind, but for this area, it did feel rather cold this year—he made his way out of the house.

His car was parked a little down the block. He was aware that if he got back too soon, his space and just about every other space, would be taken, but right now, all Keith could focus on was making a successful escape.

He thought he could slip out unnoticed, but he should have known better.

Apparently Clumsy Mac had developed eyes in the back of her head as well as what amounted to a sixth sense.

As he tried to leave, she called out to him, asking him a question that made absolutely no sense to him. "So, are you going to go out to look for a tree?"

Completely baffled by her question, he turned around to look at Kenzie. Several people in the immediate area, he noticed, appeared to be invested in this possible exchange between them. But given that she was ringing up sales and surrounded by people, he couldn't very well take her aside to ask her what she was talking about.

He did his best to ignore the others, mostly women, listening in as he crossed over to her and asked, "Come again?"

"A tree," she repeated, enunciating the words slowly. "Are you going out to look for a tree?"

"Why would I want to look for a tree? There are trees all over the place here."

Kenzie smiled at him, and he caught himself wondering how a smile could be both sensually appealing and damn annoying at the same time.

"A Christmas tree," Kenzie specified.

Okay, now she was either kidding or she'd lost her mind, Keith concluded.

"I can't think of a single reason why I'd want to go out to buy a Christmas tree, of all things." His tone was dismissive as he turned to walk to his car.

Kenzie quickly made her way around the long table to reach him. "I'll be right back," she promised the person who was about to be rung up. Catching up to Keith, she took hold of his arm so that she could slow his pace. "Mrs. Sommers said that it would help with the sale of the house."

Keith frowned as he tried to remember the real estate agent telling him that. This was news to him. "When did she say that?" he questioned, giving Kenzie the benefit of the doubt.

"She mentioned it to me when she gave me the details about this job. She said that houses were hard to sell this time of year because kids are in school and the holidays are coming up. But according to her, the one thing that helps sell a house even around Christmas is highlighting the season, emphasizing that warm, fuzzy, greeting card commercial kind of thing. Ergo, getting a really terrific Christmas tree and displaying it in a prominent place in the house."

He couldn't believe he was hearing her correctly. A house was a house. It was either a good buy or it wasn't. How was adding what amounted to disposable ginger-bread supposed to change that?

"You're serious?" he asked in disbelief, giving her the opportunity to recant.

"Are you serious about selling the house?"

To his credit, he managed to contain his impatience. "Yes."

"Then I'm serious. It's not my suggestion," she pointed out. "It was hers."

A wave of frustration washed over him. "I don't even know where to find an artificial tree," Keith began.

It had been ages since he'd even had a Christmas tree. The last time was roughly ten years ago, in his dorm room. He didn't bother celebrating the season these days. Once Amy was gone, Christmas had ceased to mean any-thing to him.

Kenzie shook her head. "No, not an artificial tree. A *real* Christmas tree," she insisted.

He blew out a breath. "Even more of a mystery," he told her.

She held up her index finger as if that would somehow hold him in his place. "Give me a few minutes."

"And you'll do what? Conjure up a Christmas tree?" he asked, only half kidding. At this point, he wasn't sure just what MacKenzie Bradshaw was capable of, but he put nothing past the woman.

"No," Kenzie told him. "I'm going to 'conjure up' re-inforcements."

If he were thinking clearly, he would have just waved a dismissive hand in her direction and gotten into his car, going in search of not a Christmas tree—that was just absurd—but some peace and quiet. Most of all, in search of some much-needed rest from all of Kenzie's seemingly never-ending, relentless cheerfulness.

He always liked to believe he was a clear thinker.

And yet, for some reason, against all logic, he stayed where he was—just as she'd asked him to.

## Chapter Ten

"Exactly who are you waiting for?" Keith asked her impatiently ten minutes later.

As he spoke, he circumvented the long display table to get on the other side, where she was standing. He knew she'd placed a call when she'd asked him to wait—and then she'd gone back to business as usual.

He turned his back to the eager-looking older woman who had just, in her words, "scored a really fantastic deal." The woman had one arm wrapped around each of the two tall, sturdy antique lamps, lamps that had stood on the nightstands that flanked his mother's bed for as far back as he could remember.

Though he had told Kenzie to get rid of everything, seeing the lamps being carried off by someone else felt decidedly strange.

With effort, he focused on the question he'd put to Kenzie and not the oddly bittersweet memory.

"Them," Kenzie answered with a touch of relief in her voice, happily pointing to someone directly behind him.

Turning around, Keith saw that Kenzie's mother and one of her sisters—the one who wasn't pregnant—were coming toward them from the curb where they'd parked a car.

Kenzie's mother smiled at him first before addressing her daughter. "Keith, how nice to see you again so soon."

If he closed his eyes, he could have sworn he'd just heard a deeper version of Kenzie's voice. "The feeling is mutual," he replied. The lawyer in him produced automatic responses.

Andrea Bradshaw turned her attention to her daughter. "You're lucky you caught us."

"Talk about giving short notice," Marilyn commented, shaking her head. "This has to be your all-time best—or worst, given your point of view."

"Desperate times, desperate measures," Kenzie said to her sister, then turned toward her mother. She paused to kiss the woman's cheek first. "Hi, Mom. Thanks for coming."

"What's so desperate?" Andrea asked. She was directing the question to her daughter but looking at Keith, making it rather obvious that she thought the source of the emergency might very well lie with him.

Without a second's hesitation, Kenzie said, "We need to go Christmas tree shopping."

Keith was about to deny her statement, saying that not only there was no need but also he wasn't about to go shopping for anything, much less a Christmas tree. He noticed that Kenzie's mother appeared to take the whole thing in stride, as did some of the women who were browsing through his mother's possessions.

Only her sister, Marilyn, appeared confused. "Come again?" she asked, giving him a very curious look.

He began to issue his denial, but Kenzie cut him off. "Long story. I'll explain later," she promised, getting her purse from a box she had tucked beneath the long table. "Besides, I knew you two miss the thrill of selling unique things." Kenzie paused to brush a quick, affectionate kiss against her mother's cheek. "We won't be gone long."

"Take as much time as you need," Andrea told her youngest, waving Kenzie on her way. "Make sure you pick a good one," she added, addressing her words to Keith before turning her attention to the next woman in line.

"The thrill of selling?" Keith echoed. With her arm through his, Kenzie was hustling him away from the driveway with its teeming buyers and eager customers and toward the light blue SUV she had driven today.

"My mother ran the business before she opted to retire and sell it to me. Marilyn worked at the store part-time when she was in college, same as me." Kenzie smiled at him over the hood of her car just before getting in. "See, I didn't leave your goods in the hands of amateurs."

He shrugged, doing his best to cling to his aloof stance. "Wouldn't matter if you did. Whatever's left, you can have some charity pick up." Getting in, he pulled the door shut and then buckled up. "Just so we're clear, I'm not looking to fund my 401-K with the net proceeds from this sale."

"We're clear," she assured him, turning on the ignition. "And just for the record, you don't have to justify anything to me. Whatever you want is fine with me."

Whatever he wanted.

Funny how that choice of words seemed to nudge thoughts into his head that hadn't been there a moment ago. Thoughts that had far more to do with this whirlwind behind the steering wheel next to him than with the business of wrapping up loose ends.

Whatever he wanted…

What if what he wanted wasn't some formless thing or a concept but something a great deal more real than that? What if he wanted to step out of the moment and into a scenario that had far more to do with the needs and desires between a man and a woman?

Between himself and Kenzie?

What was going on with him? The woman was talking about his mother's possessions, not about anything personal.

Maybe this concept of not having any ties to anyone was getting to him, and subconsciously he was trying to make a connection, *any* connection.

Could that be why he suddenly found himself having feelings *for* and feelings *about* Kenzie?

Ridiculous. He didn't have feelings for Kenzie, he silently insisted. He needed to get a grip.

What he really needed was to be away from her, not confined with her in a space that was smaller than the average closet.

He had to get out.

"Look, why don't you just drop me off somewhere and go on ahead by yourself?" he suggested, scanning the area they were passing to see if it looked familiar to him.

Kenzie spared him a glance as she quickly squeezed through a yellow light. "And why would I want to do something like that?"

"Because you have more experience at this tree-buying thing than I do, and you obviously like the idea of shopping for a Christmas tree." Shifting so that he could reach the wallet in his pocket, he wrapped his fingers around the smooth leather and extracted it. "You can get two of them. One for yourself—my treat," he emphasized, producing two hundred-dollar bills.

"You're too late," she told him, amused.

"You've already got a tree?" he guessed, surprised.

Kenzie looked at him as if she couldn't believe he was actually asking the question. "Christmas is in a few days. Of course I have a tree."

"Of course," he echoed.

The words were no sooner out of his mouth than he had to brace his hands against the dashboard to keep from leaning into her. Kenzie had taken a sharp turn into a parking lot. It was located before a cluster of stores. A supermarket filled up more than half of that area.

"Why are we—? Oh." Keith had started to ask why they were stopping here, but then he saw the answer.

There, in a roped-off section before the entrance to the grocery store, was a collection of Christmas trees of varying sizes. They were clustered over to one side, each apparently in need of a good home. At least, that's what he assumed she'd say to him if he happened to ask.

Kenzie turned off the engine, unbuckled her seat belt and slid out of her seat. She was about to close her door when she saw that he still hadn't budged.

"Well, c'mon," she urged. "The tree isn't about to select itself and jump onto our roof. We have to single it out and pay for it first."

This whole trip was silly. It only made him acutely aware of the fact that being in an enclosed space with Kenzie aroused him, which was just about the very last thing in the world he wanted.

"You know, having a tree in the living room or wherever isn't going to sell the house any faster," he told her cynically.

"Maybe not, but not having one might just send a bad

message to the prospective buyer about the so-called 'vi-brations' that came with the house," she told him. "Trust me, you need to do just about everything you can to tip the scales in your favor. And it never hurts to take your agent's advice. Real estate can be a rather a cutthroat competition at times."

Maybe she had a point, after all. In any event, they were here. Shrugging, he said, "Sure, why not? I'll get a tree. Anything else? Warm kittens? A fuzzy puppy?"

"If you had a fuzzy puppy, that wouldn't hurt, but it's too late to get one and try to train it to respond to you on cue for the buyers' benefit. That sort of thing always back-fires. But having a pretty Christmas tree should do the trick," she assured him. "Not to mention that putting the tree up and decorating it might just cheer you up, as well."

His back went up automatically. "Who says I need cheering up?" he asked. When she started to laugh, he decided to drop that line of questioning. But she'd also said something else he couldn't just ignore. "What do you mean, 'decorating'?" he asked.

"Decorations. You know, balls, garland, some tinsel." She paused, looking at him, waiting for the light to dawn or, barring that, the frown to fade. When it didn't, she asked, "What part of that don't you understand?"

"The part where I'm the one doing it," Keith answered bluntly. "I don't decorate Christmas trees," he informed her flatly.

"Ever?" she questioned incredulously. She remembered Amy talking about the ritual that had been involved in decorating her family Christmas tree. One day just for setting the tree up, two days for the lights and then one day for all the rest of the decorations. Her friend had never indicated that Keith wasn't part of this tradition.

"Not in the last ten years."

It seemed to her that everything of any true meaning in Keith's life had come to an abrupt stop with his sister's death. Her heart ached for him.

"Then maybe it's about time you got back in the game," she told him gently.

Though he got out of the vehicle, he felt wounds opening up. Old, painful wounds. "Why? Because you say so?"

"No, because it's the right thing to do," she answered quietly.

He looked at Kenzie pointedly. She was trying to manipulate his life. What gave her the right? "According to?"

"Everybody," she answered without hesitation. "Don't resist so hard," Kenzie gently cajoled, treating him with kid gloves. "Why not put that energy toward getting the job done?"

He knew exactly what he wanted to do with that energy, and putting up a Christmas tree was not it.

Even so, he fell into step beside her as they went to look at potential Christmas trees. But he didn't want her to think that it wasn't under protest. "I'll help you get a tree, but I'm not decorating it."

"Uh-huh." Kenzie smiled.

"About time you got back," were the first words out of Marilyn's mouth when she saw her sister and Keith getting out of Kenzie's vehicle. "I was beginning to give up hope."

"Don't let her snow you," Andrea spoke up, handing a young boy who had just bought his mother a Christmas present his change. "She's been having the time of her life."

Marilyn tossed her head, her hair bouncing against her shoulders. "That's because I'm such a good actress."

Andrea ignored her older daughter's play for sympathy. She smiled warmly as she scrutinized the fruits of Kenzie and Keith's hunt.

"I see you got the tree. Very nice," she approved. "Marilyn and I can stay on out here while you decorate it."

Marilyn groaned, then murmured, "Sorry," to the woman in front of her who was examining an intricately carved vase.

Kenzie laughed. "That's okay, Mom. You and Marilyn have done more than enough. The tree'll keep. Keith and I can decorate it after we close up for the day."

Her comment surprised Keith. He thought that this argument had been settled earlier when they had gone looking for this damn Christmas tree she'd been so set on finding. He really should have known better. "Wait, what?"

"The tree can keep for a few hours," she said to him before turning back to her mother. "I can take over now, Mom. And thanks for all your help," she added with sincerity. Turning toward her sister, she said, "You, too, Marilyn."

Her sister muttered something unintelligible in response. Kenzie knew better than to ask Marilyn to repeat it.

The first day of the estate sale lasted until the appointed time on the flyers she'd posted around the development: five o'clock. At exactly one minute after five, Kenzie tendered her regrets to the handful of stragglers left, promising to reopen the estate sale in two days, at which time the remaining items would be available.

"Why not tomorrow?" one woman asked.

Aware that Keith might be within earshot, Kenzie worded her answer carefully. "The lady who owned this house is being buried tomorrow. It wouldn't seem right to hold the sale during her funeral."

"Oh." The single word was laced with contrition and unspoken apologies.

"Thank you for your business, ladies," Kenzie announced, officially closing down the sale.

She waited for the women to leave the driveway and make their way to their vehicles. Satisfied that the last of the potential customers had left the premises, Kenzie began to pack up the items that still hadn't sold.

As she tucked them into boxes she'd kept under the tables, she was surprised, not to mention pleased, to have Keith pitch in. He began putting the remaining items away without saying a single word.

"You don't have to do this," she told him. This was really her job, not his. That had been part of the initial arrangement.

"It'll go faster this way," he responded.

Finished packing, he realized that she was planning on closing up the tables and putting them into the garage for the time being. He was about to tell her to leave them out when it occurred to him that she wanted them cleared away because of the funeral reception tomorrow. She seemed more concerned about decorum than he was.

Blowing out a breath, he got on one side of the table and pushed after she'd removed the extension, closing the section so that the table was one half its original size. Done, he dragged the table into the garage, then closed it.

"Thanks," she told him, flashing the smile that he caught himself looking forward to seeing.

"No problem. Does that get me out of decorating that thing?" he asked, nodding at the house. They'd carried in the Christmas tree earlier.

"If you really don't want to decorate the tree, you don't have to. I can do it by myself." It was a simple statement of fact and not punctuated with a pout.

He eyed her suspiciously and shook his head.

"What's the matter?" she asked him.

"I'm beginning to know you. You don't give up that easily."

"I'm not giving up, but I certainly can't strong-arm you into doing it," she pointed out. "That would be physically impossible." She paused before adding, "But I do think you should decorate the tree."

"Why?" he challenged her. He sensed that he was doomed and that he'd wind up decorating this tree, but he wanted her to work for it.

"Think of it as a tribute to your mother," she urged him. "The women coming back from the funeral will find it very touching that you went out of your way like this to keep the magic of Christmas alive for her even though she's not here to enjoy it anymore."

His face darkened. "Why would I want to pay tribute to a woman who dropped out of life? Who was so fixated on her pain, she didn't notice that anyone else was in pain, as well?"

So that was it, Kenzie thought. He hadn't forgiven his mother for not being there for him after Amy had died. He'd been hurting and his mother didn't reach out to him. Instead, she was trying to find a way to deal with her own pain. Both of them had been isolated without realizing that the key to everything lay within each other.

"Because she's your mother," Kenzie insisted, trying to break through the wall he'd constructed around himself once and for all.

"Maybe that's not enough of a reason," Keith fired back.

"Well, it's going to have to be," she told him matter-of-factly.

With that, Kenzie left the driveway. After a beat, Keith followed her inside, albeit exceedingly reluctantly.

He would ignore her. If she wanted to spout nonsense and pretend that decorating a tree was going to change anything, that was her problem. Nowhere did it say that he had to decorate the Christmas tree he had been forced to buy.

He certainly didn't have to stay in the same room and watch her do it, either.

Just because he still didn't feel like going into any of the other rooms after all these years didn't mean he had to hang around the living room, watching Kenzie struggle with Christmas lights that always seemed to be knotted up no matter how carefully they had been put away the previous year.

He could go anywhere he wanted to.

Somehow, like a moth to a flame, he still managed to wind up staying in the living room.

Standing beside the tree that was still bundled up and lying on the floor, Kenzie could *sense* that he was behind her. She glanced over her shoulder to see that he was just inside the room's threshold. But that didn't mean he was going to help her.

Kenzie worked with what she had. "Have you decided to supervise?" she asked.

The sound of her voice broke through the jumble of thoughts that were circling around his brain, as tangled as the Christmas lights always were, year after year.

"What? No, I haven't decided anything," he answered. At this point he was just trying to resist offering to help her decorate the tree for as long as he could.

"Because you could, you know," she went on, slowly drawing him in. "That way you could be part of it without having to compromise any of whatever principles you feel you're trying to maintain in this battle of dueling philosophies."

Coming closer to her, Keith shook his head as if to clear it. "You know, sometimes I don't understand a word you're saying."

Kenzie laughed, the warm sound wrapping itself around him. "That's okay. Sometimes I don't, either. But what I'm trying to tell you right now is that you can still maintain your distance—if that's what you want—but be part of this by telling me where you want me to put the various ornaments. This way, the tree'll get decorated with your help, but without you having to touch any of the decorations."

"I have nothing against the actual touching of decorations," he protested.

"Okay, if that's how you feel, wonderful. Touch away," she encouraged him.

He looked at her, then started to laugh. "Do you have any idea how crazy that sounds?"

"Maybe," she conceded. "But it got you to laugh, didn't it?"

That was when he realized his laughter had been her goal all along. "Okay, you win. I'll decorate the tree with you."

The exceedingly pleased expression on her face more than took the sting out of his surrender.

## Chapter Eleven

"You do realize that I don't know where anything is?" Keith asked her the next moment.

He glanced at the tree lying on the floor, still tightly bound up like the hostage of Christmas Past. He'd made his peace with decorating it—he was here, Kenzie was here, the tree was here, and he had some time to kill, so what would it ultimately hurt? But the practical problem that now confronted him and this relentless Christmas elf beside him was the unknown location of these decorations.

"And by 'anything' you mean...?" Kenzie let her voice trail off, waiting for him to elaborate.

"I mean the tree stand, the ornaments and whatever else that thing—" he waved a hand at the tree on the floor behind him "—requires."

He had to admit that he expected Kenzie to throw in the towel when faced with this news. He didn't expect her to flash that dazzling grin of hers and then shoot down his eleventh-hour glimmer of hope. "That's okay. I do."

*Of course you do*, he commented silently. Out loud he voiced his natural skepticism. If he didn't know where the decorations were kept, why would she? "How would you know?"

Her mesmerizing grin turned into a patient smile. "I took inventory, remember?" Then, before he could question anything further, she volunteered the ornaments' location. "The decorations are in your pull-down attic. As for the tree stand, that's in the corner in the garage behind the black plastic box of wires and extension cords," she informed him cheerfully.

He knew he'd agreed to do this with her, but he wouldn't have forgiven himself if he hadn't given this one last try. "Look, if the decorations are all tucked away, why don't we just leave them there?"

Kenzie didn't even blink—or accuse him of reneging. "Because then the tree'll stay naked. Since we bought the tree—"

"And whose idea was that?" Keith reminded her pointedly.

Kenzie blissfully continued making her argument, pretending to take no notice that he had interjected anything. "It might as well be decorated," she stubbornly concluded.

The last time he'd been in that attic, Amy had been filling out applications to different colleges. The memory brought a bitter pang to his heart.

"And you expect me to climb up into the attic and get the decorations," Keith assumed.

"Expect?" she echoed and then shook her head. "No. I don't put demands on people," Kenzie told him just before she left the room.

Now what? Was this a show of temper? "Where are you going?" he called after Kenzie.

Rather than returning, Kenzie just raised her voice so he could hear her answer. "Well, since I haven't figured out how to make decorations come when I call them, I guess I'm going into the attic to get them."

The next second, he heard the door leading into the garage open and then close again. Kenzie had left the house.

"Darned woman," Keith muttered under his breath, hurrying after her.

He walked into the garage just in time to see Kenzie lowering the folded ladder that led up into the attic. Balancing it, she pulled at the rung to extend the ladder.

"Move out of the way," he told her gruffly just as she snapped the locks on either side of the ladder into place, strengthening it.

She wasn't sure what Keith intended to do, and she wanted to get on with decorating the tree. "But—"

"Don't argue with me," he ordered. Taking hold of both her shoulders, Keith literally moved her to the side, giving him clear access to the attic's entrance above.

"I wouldn't dream of it," she responded. She punctuated the innocent statement with an equally innocent smile.

He wasn't taken in for a second. Kenzie had orchestrated this, he thought.

"Ha!" The single word echoed behind him as he climbed up the ladder.

"Don't forget to flip on the light," she called up after Keith. She positioned herself at the base of the ladder so she could take the various boxes from him as he handed them down one at a time.

"Whose attic is this, anyway?" he retorted.

"Yours," she answered as if he was actually asking her

a serious question. "I just thought that after all these years, you might have forgotten about the light in the attic."

Maybe he had forgotten, Keith thought as he stood on the top rung of the ladder, looking around the dimly lit enclosure. Forgotten about the light—it still worked. Most of all, forgotten there were vivid memories attached to the things tucked away up here. Memories that in turn stirred bittersweet feelings within him, slicing through him like the whirling blades of a helicopter.

Kenzie shifted from foot to foot as she looked up the ladder. "Do you see them?" she asked, raising her voice so that he could hear her. He was being too quiet.

"Yes, I see them," he answered, more to himself than to her.

This was a bad idea, Keith thought again. But he couldn't very well say anything because he didn't want Kenzie to think he was affected. He wanted her to believe that he could remain detached from all this. Her sympathy would be too much for him to take right now.

He especially didn't want her pity. Toughing this out was the only way he could keep up the image he was trying to hang on to. If he allowed his emotions to engulf him, he had no idea where it would all end up.

But it would be no place good.

"Do you want me to go up to help you?" Kenzie offered.

Was it his imagination, or had her voice softened a little? Keith stiffened, as if that could ward off any unwanted sentiment coming his way.

"The attic doesn't have enough room for two of us," Keith bit out. "Not with all this stuff crammed into it."

He didn't remember there being so many decorations. But then, he'd tried not to remember anything because initially, it had just been too painful for him. Amy's death had almost shattered him. She'd been the vital, happy one, the one who never became discouraged, no matter what.

After a while, not remembering was a better way to go for him. It was just easier to wipe his memory clean and pretend there hadn't been small, loving Christmases filled with laughter if not with presents.

"If you come down," Kenzie said, "then I can go up instead and you don't have to—"

He turned just enough to look down at her from his elevated position near the top of the ladder. "Do you *ever* stop talking?" he asked.

Kenzie treated it like a serious question, pretending she didn't hear the sorrow threatening to break through in his voice. "I do, on occasion."

"Can this be one of those occasions?" It wasn't really a question so much as a request.

Kenzie bit the inside of her bottom lip and really struggled not to say anything further. Not because she was insulted—she wasn't—but because in Keith's present state, although it went against everything she normally felt compelled to do, she had a feeling that silence would be easier for him to bear than bright, cheerful chatter.

He wasn't in a place right now where he would respond positively to banter.

So she stood at the bottom of the ladder, quietly waiting for Keith to hand one of the plastic containers of decorations down.

She'd almost given up hope that he actually would when Keith finally lowered the first box of silver-and-blue ornaments to her. He descended just enough rungs to cut the distance between them so that when she extended her arms up, she was able to take hold of the box.

Kenzie rose up on her toes as far as she could as she stretched her arms, angling so that he wouldn't have to

bend down too far. The look Keith gave her silently told
her she was trying too hard. Being Kenzie, she deliberately ignored the message. She was just happy that he'd
come around enough to begin bringing down the decorations.

*Every journey starts with the first step*, she thought,
heartened.

The prolonged process of retrieving the decorations
and handing them down the ladder lasted close to an hour.
And once all the boxes were finally down, Kenzie turned
her attention to the tree stand.

"I'm going to get some food and water ready for the
tree, and then I'll need help getting the tree into the
stand," she told Keith.

He frowned. "Food and water? Room service for a
Christmas tree?" he questioned, looking at her as if she'd
lost her mind.

"The tree's a living thing," Kenzie reminded him.
"Every living thing requires at least water. Most require
water *and* food. Plant food," she explained, patting her
skirt pocket. She took a packet out of it to show him.
"When we bought the tree, the guy at the lot gave me
this. He said it helps the tree last until after the holidays."

Keith shook his head, negating her plans. "It doesn't
have to last until after the holidays. As far as I'm concerned, it doesn't have to last longer than a few days.
After that, I'm out of here and the tree winds up on the
garbage heap, waiting for collection."

She'd really been hoping that all this would have gotten him to change his mind, to stay awhile and at least
begin to work through the anger and sadness she saw in
his eyes. But he seemed determined to remain unhappy,
to hang on to all those issues clearly haunting him.

"Then you are leaving right after the reception?" she asked quietly.

He did his best remain removed from her tone and not allow it to get to him. He deliberately blocked out the sadness he heard. "I'd be leaving right after the funeral if someone hadn't insisted on holding a reception right afterward."

She let that comment pass. There was no point in going into it now. Instead, she approached the situation logically. "It'll be late then. Why not fly out in the morning, when you're fresh?"

The first thing that came to him was to say that he wanted to leave Bedford behind him as soon as possible, but she had been very cheerful and upbeat about all this extra work and without complaint—never mind that he hadn't asked for it. He owed Kenzie, even if he didn't say so.

Keith supposed a few more hours here wouldn't make that much difference. "Maybe I will," he conceded.

Kenzie had already cleared away all the boxes he had handed down to her, taking them into the family room. When Keith came down the ladder with the last load, she took that box from him and quickly brought it into the house to join the others. By the time he had the ladder folding into itself and then neatly retracting into the ceiling, she was digging the tree stand out of the corner.

"About that help I asked for," she began tactfully, holding the stand aloft.

Keith's response was a sigh, but he didn't turn her down or even offer any excuses.

Following her into the house, he looked down at the offending blue spruce. "Might as well get this over with," he muttered, resigned. "Where do you want it?" he asked her.

Kenzie looked around the family room slowly, as if she had a vision.

"Where did you used to put the tree?" she asked.

Keith shrugged dismissively. "I don't know," he responded irritably, then shrugged again. "Anywhere."

She placed the stand down by the window, then looked over toward him. "Here?" It was a question, not a suggestion.

*What did it matter?* He didn't want it here to begin with. "Good a place as any," he responded.

"You really don't remember?" Kenzie asked incredulously.

Yes, he remembered. "It was the middle of the room," Keith bit out, glaring at her. "Happy now?"

Kenzie didn't answer that one way or the other. What she did say was "Thank you," followed by what he could only describe as a sweet, completely guileless smile.

The polite answer made him ashamed of his testiness and the temper he'd allowed to flare. But the woman was trying too hard to recreate something dead and not about to be resurrected.

Still, Keith told himself, he didn't have to be so curt. Apparently Kenzie couldn't help being a pain in the neck.

He blew out a breath, then murmured, "I didn't mean to bite your head off like that. Sorry."

Kenzie moved her head from side to side as if she were actually testing her neck to make sure it was all right. "Still attached," she announced with a wide grin that reached her eyes. "No harm done." With that, she moved the stand into the middle of the room. "Just help me get the tree into the stand and then I won't bother you anymore."

Keith laughed shortly. "Yeah, right. Like I believe that," he said, resurrecting his facade.

Even so, he picked the tree up from the floor and carried it, still bound, over to the stand.

He moved so quickly, he caught her off guard. Kenzie hurried over to him as he carried the tree. "Wait, let me help with that."

He refrained from saying that she'd only get in his way if she tried to carry the tree with him. "You just hold the stand still," Keith told her. "I'll handle the tree."

Kenzie could tell by his voice that he was straining. It made her feel guilty in addition to useless. "The tree's heavy," she insisted.

She knew that despite the fact that when they had carried it into the house together, she had brought up the top while he had picked up the bottom part before she could say anything. The angle he employed while carrying it assured him that the brunt of the weight was on his end. Even so, she could tell that the tree was more than a little on the heavy side.

"Nothing gets past you, does it?" Keith commented sarcastically, holding the tree still.

Kenzie had dropped to her knees and was moving as quickly as she could, tightening the stand's screws into place. The tricky part was making sure that all three screws were equally tightened, keeping the tree carefully balanced between them. She knew this couldn't be easy for him, keeping the spruce perfectly upright the way he was. "I should have called my brothers to come help."

"And I should have called the airlines and booked an earlier flight, but none of that's happening, so let's just work with what we've got, okay?" he told her, trying not to raise his voice. "Have you finished adjusting the screws yet?"

Kenzie shuffled around the perimeter. "Almost," she answered.

It felt as if she was vainly turning the screws, getting nowhere. And then, after what felt like an eternity, she couldn't move any of the three screws even half a turn further.

"Okay, test it," she told him, snaking her way back out from under the tree.

Rocking back on her heels, Kenzie took in a deep breath. Her first unobstructed one in a while, or so it felt.

Remaining somewhat skeptical, Keith slowly tested the tree's stability by partially releasing one of his hands from around its trunk.

The second he felt the tree beginning to list, he quickly closed his hand around the trunk again, holding it tightly. He'd never let go with his other hand.

"Not good enough," he told her.

Kenzie blew out a breath that sounded suspiciously more like a deep sigh.

"You liked saying that, didn't you?" It wasn't an accusation but an observation.

Keith inclined his head as if conceding the point. "It had its appeal."

Keith was fighting her every step of the way—but he was also ultimately going along with it, she noted happily. And that was the bottom line.

Inside all that bravado and aloof rhetoric he so liberally dispensed, there was a man who still cared. A man who did his best to appear distant and removed, but who was really the opposite upon closer examination.

And *that* was the man whom she wanted to reach, the one she wanted to extend her hand to and hold on tightly to so that he knew he wasn't alone.

Because she was there for him. And intended to be for as long as he needed her.

"Done yet?" Keith demanded as she once again moved

around the tree, reworking the three screws, trying to get a more equitable distribution of the tree's weight.

She didn't answer him immediately. Not until she'd tightened the last screw and satisfied herself that there was no way the base could possibly still wiggle.

"Done!" Kenzie finally declared in much the same voice that competing cowboys in a rodeo used when they'd secured the steer they had roped and brought down.

She crawled out from underneath the tree for a second time, her face somewhat flushed. Keith caught himself staring at the way the color infused her cheeks.

The next second, he roused himself and let go of the tree.

For a one long moment, the tree appeared to be almost perfect. The next, it began to list again, this time ever so slightly to one side.

Keith sighed. Then he looked at her face and knew exactly what she was thinking.

"It doesn't have to be perfect," he told her. "After all, it's just a tree."

Kenzie fisted her hands on her hips and gave him a look that he dreaded getting from teachers back in school.

"A *Christmas* tree," she corrected him, implying that made all the difference in the world. "And yes, it does. You give up too easy, O'Connell. Hold the tree," she ordered.

With that, Kenzie got back down on her hands and knees for the third time, crawled under the tree on her stomach and went back to work.

The woman, Keith thought as he held the tree as still as he could, was stubbornness personified.

He didn't realize, at least not immediately, that he was smiling as he thought it.

## Chapter Twelve

"Okay, you proved your point," Keith conceded in grudging admiration.

It had taken Kenzie another fifteen minutes of adjusting and readjusting, but the Christmas tree they had brought into his house, looming at approximately seven and a half feet without taking the stand into account, was finally perfectly straight.

"You did it. The tree's straight. Your job is done," he pronounced.

"The tree's straight," Kenzie agreed, dusting herself off. "But the job's far from done yet." When she saw Keith arch a quizzical brow in her direction, she explained, "The decorations you brought down are still in their boxes. Job's not done until they're on the tree."

Keith shook his head as he blew out an impatient breath. "You're relentless, aren't you?"

Her smile rose into her eyes, highlighting her amusement at his assessment.

"I take vitamins," she quipped. "Don't worry," she was quick to assure him. "I'm not going to rope you into helping me. You can go do whatever it is you were planning on doing."

The fact was, he had no plans, other than to knock back a stiff drink or two to help relax him enough so that, with luck, he could fall asleep. The funeral was tomorrow, and although he told himself that he wasn't viewing the event emotionally, he was utterly wired about having to be there tomorrow.

He felt like a spring that would release at any second with just the slightest touch. That wasn't a good state to be in, he silently lectured himself.

She was brushing off the last of tiny, fuzzy lint that was clinging to the front of her light blue sweater. For just a fleeting moment, he envisioned his own fingers brushing it away.

Keith forced himself to focus on the moment instead. "Why are you doing this?" he asked her suddenly.

She never missed a beat as she answered, "Because a Christmas tree needs Christmas decorations. Otherwise, it's just a tree in the house that's lost its way."

Keith laughed under his breath as he shook his head. "Do you think these things up, or do they just come to you?"

She opened the first box and took out five decorations, depicting a family of colorfully dressed mice that appeared to have stepped right out of a children's cartoon. "How cute," she murmured under her breath.

Attaching a hook to each, she hung one decoration from each finger on her left hand, then turned toward the tree.

"If you're going to talk, grab a decoration," she told him.

"I thought you weren't going to rope me into helping

you," he reminded her even as he picked a gleaming mul-
tiplaned silver decoration out of the box closest to him.
The decoration cast a shower of rainbows as the light hit
it. For just a moment, it threatened to stir an old memory,
but he suppressed it.

"I don't see any rope," she replied, pretending to scan
the immediate area before she turned an innocent face
up to him. "Do you?"

"I stand corrected," he conceded wryly. He watched
as she distributed the decorations in her hand, hanging
them on different branches. "So why are you doing this?
The truth," he specified.

Kenzie spared him one glance over her shoulder before taking out another five decorations and repeating
her procedure.

"Other than the fact that I love Christmas trees?" she
asked.

He was trying to get to the unvarnished truth, convinced that people didn't go out of their way for other
people without an ulterior motive. "Other than that," he
prodded.

Hanging the last decorations, she went back for re-
placements. She didn't have to think about her answer. It
was something that had always guided her.

"Because it's a nice touch. Because it pulls a thread of
continuity through what's happening. People leave us,"
she added in a more quiet voice, as if she would ever get
used to the reality of that fact.

"You mean they die," he clarified.

She didn't like that word, never had. "They leave us,"
she continued doggedly. "But the traditions they leave
behind continue, just like life."

"That's a lovely philosophy," he told her flippantly.
She was on shaky ground in his opinion. She couldn't

back that up with any amount of certainty. "How do you know my mother didn't stop celebrating Christmas right after Amy died?" he asked.

Kenzie paused, her hand hovering over the next box of decorations. There was a quiet certainty in her voice when she answered him. "She would have celebrated twice as hard, for Amy as well as for herself."

Kenzie was right—and he'd never understood why his mother had been so adamant about going all out that way. The holiday had lost all its meaning for him. Because Amy had always somehow been at the center of the celebration. She'd been the one who bridged any flares of temper that erupted between his mother and him.

Keith hung the decoration and then, for a moment, he contemplated just walking out of the room and leaving her to decorate the tree by herself.

But all this talk about the holiday had him thinking of Amy. With an inward sigh, he picked up another decoration, knowing Amy would have wanted him to.

"How did you know?" he asked in a low voice after a beat.

"I didn't, not definitively," she qualified. "It's just a feeling. I'd do the same thing myself in her place." She could see that Keith still didn't understand. "Celebrating that way helped your mother keep Amy's memory alive, made her feel that Amy was still there with her," she explained. "With both of you."

Stepping back to view their progress so far, Kenzie realized her oversight.

"Help me with the ladder," she told him, heading into the garage. "We forgot to put the star on the top."

Keith gave the tree a quick once-over. "Instead of dragging in the ladder, why don't you just leave the star off?" he suggested. "Looks fine without one."

Kenzie frowned. "It looks naked without a star," she insisted. The next moment, she reversed her position. After all, he'd gone along with the rest of it. Maybe he'd respond better if she cut him a break. "Okay, the star doesn't have to go on. But I still need to decorate the upper part of the tree." With that, she went into the garage.

Keith followed right behind her.

"That's too heavy," he told her, taking possession of the ladder.

"I'm stronger than I look," Kenzie protested, although she did like the fact that he was bringing the ladder into the house.

"You're also more annoying than you look," he countered as he brought the ladder into the family room. He set it up beside the tree.

Kenzie made no response to his comment. Instead, she took out another five decorations. By the time he turned around to face her, she had made her way up the ladder and was one step from the top.

Biting off a curse, Keith quickly circled around the ladder to get to her side of it. One hand braced against the top of the ladder, Kenzie was stretching to hang the decorations as high as she could place them.

Keith grabbed hold of the ladder on either side to steady it. "Are you trying to break your fool neck?" he accused her.

"Not particularly," she answered as if he'd asked a legitimate question. Her hold on the ladder's top rung tightened as she felt it sway ever so slightly beneath her. "But I just might if you grab the ladder like that again."

Choice words rose to his lips, but Keith managed to refrain from saying them. Instead, he told her, "Why don't you come down and I'll do that?"

As if he really wanted to, she thought, feeling there

was only so far she could push him before he just walked out. "No, that's okay. I—"

"I said come down." This time it wasn't a suggestion but an order, uttered through clenched teeth as he glared up at her.

She debated arguing with him, then decided having Keith insist like that was a good thing. It meant that he was involved in the process, at least for the moment.

"Coming down," she announced agreeably, making her way down the ladder.

The moment she had both feet back on the floor, Keith moved her out of the way and took Kenzie's place on the ladder.

In general, he wasn't as quick as she was when it came to hanging up decorations, or as limber when it came to running up and down the ladder, so the job wound up taking longer. But eventually, the upper half of the tree was finished.

As was, he noted, the bottom half of the tree. Kenzie had quietly emulated his progress by hanging up decorations on the bottom half of the tree, covering an equal amount of ground in about half the time. The entire tree was finished.

"Not bad," he grudgingly murmured.

"Not bad?" Kenzie echoed incredulously. "Why, it's beautiful!" she declared with feeling.

Keith merely shrugged, determined to sound far less enthusiastic, even though the truth was he'd enjoyed doing this with her. But if Kenzie caught a hint of that, he was certain that he would not hear the end of it, not until his plane finally took off.

"At least it's done," he said carelessly. "I'm beat. Unless you've got some magical trip to Neverland up your sleeve, I'm turning in." He looked her way, waiting for some last-minute pitch.

"There's been enough magic for one day," she told him. Maybe he was just exhausted and imagining things, but he could have sworn he saw her eyes gleaming. The next minute, she managed to catch him off guard again. "I'll be here in the morning," Kenzie told him as she gathered together her things.

He tried to make sense of what she'd just said. "I'm going to the funeral," he reminded her.

Kenzie slipped her purse onto her shoulder. "I know. I'm going, too."

He stared at Kenzie. He hadn't come right out and extended an invitation to her, so he had just assumed she wasn't attending. Was she doing it out of some misguided sense of obligation—or worse, out of pity?

He felt his back going up.

"You don't have to," he told Kenzie stiffly.

"I know that," she answered. Flashing a smile at him, she declared, "The tree looks great. See you tomorrow at eight."

With that, Kenzie went out the door, pulling it shut behind her.

Shaking his head, Keith flipped the front door's lock into place. Then, feeling close to exhausted, he went up to his old bedroom. He'd changed out of his clothes and had climbed into bed before he realized that he'd forgotten to have those two shots of scotch he'd initially wanted to help him unwind.

It was the last thing he thought of before he fell asleep.

It seemed as if he had just closed his eyes before he was opening them again. But night had come and gone, and now the blush of daylight was just beginning to make its way into his room.

With daylight came the ambivalent feelings he was too groggy to bury effectively yet. They loomed over him like monsters that had slipped out of his childhood closet.

Part of him wanted to skip the funeral entirely. His mother hadn't been there for him the past ten years of his life, he thought angrily. Why should he be there for her when she was being buried?

But if he didn't attend the funeral, he had a very strong feeling that Kenzie would come and find him. He wouldn't put it past her to drag him to the service, literally. He no longer felt he could place any limits on what the woman was capable of, or her tenacity, for that matter.

So with the greatest reluctance, Keith forced himself out of bed, showered, shaved and made himself presentable.

He stared at the man in the mirror, who was staring back at him with eyes that appeared hollow. He was as braced as he figured he could be to face this ordeal.

He might have been braced, but he discovered that he wasn't all that ready for it. When the doorbell rang a few minutes later, he all but jumped out of his skin as the sound echoed around him.

Keith came hurrying down the stairs. He reached the front door just as he heard the doorbell ring for a third time.

"Ghosts don't ring doorbells," she said.

It was the first thing Kenzie saw when the door opened, how very pale he looked. She took a quick guess as to the reason for his lack of color. The smile on her lips was neither teasing nor amused. It was understanding.

"I know that," he said curtly, congratulating himself that he hadn't actually snapped at her.

Kenzie appeared to take no offense at his tone. "Just something I thought I'd pass on," she told him glibly. And then she grew more serious as she looked him over again. "Are you going to be all right?"

The concern in her voice, which he equated to pity, helped lift him out of the emotional hole he'd suddenly fallen into.

"I'll be fine," he all but bit out.

Kenzie quickly assessed the situation. It sounded to her as if he wouldn't allow himself to give in to any emotional triggers. Apparently he would be a brick wall.

But even brick walls cracked if enough pressure was applied.

"Of course you will," Kenzie agreed, her voice chipper.

"That means you don't have to come," he told her pointedly, repeating what he'd said to her last night.

"I know I don't have to," she continued in the same agreeable tone, except that this time, she was more forceful. "But I *want* to." There was quiet resolution in her voice.

He inclined his head, knowing there was no arguing with her. If he was being honest with himself, he was grateful for her unspoken support.

"As long as it's your choice," he told her. "I'm not about to turn you away." The warm feeling he was experiencing told him just how grateful he was that she had elected to stick it out, no matter what he'd said to try to make her leave.

However, he wasn't about to admit his gratitude to Kenzie. If she knew how he felt, that might jeopardize things between them, throw them off balance. He didn't want to risk it.

The church was already close to packed when they arrived. Finding a parking space proved to be a challenge, and he had to circle the parking lot on both sides of the church before he found a spot.

Finding a pew would have been equally as difficult except that the first one had been reserved for the deceased's family. He was the only mourner who could lay claim to that. His father hadn't been in the picture for a very long time, and his mother had no siblings. With Amy gone, he was the only family member left.

In a move that was completely unplanned, he led Kenzie behind him as he slid into the pew.

Just before he took his seat, Keith was surprised to see that members of her family—the same people he had met for the first time only two days ago—were in the church, as well, clustered together in the next few pews. That meant they had been sitting there for a while now.

Lowering his head, he whispered to Kenzie, "Why is your family here?"

Kenzie looked over her shoulder and smiled at her mother before answering. "They're here in order to show support."

"But they didn't know my mother." At least, as far as he knew, none of them did.

The next moment, Kenzie confirmed his assumption. "No, but they know you."

It still didn't make any sense to him. "Does that mean that you strong-armed them into attending the funeral?" He wouldn't have put it past her.

But Kenzie shook her head. "No. I didn't have to. I'm the youngest. I learned from them, not the other way around. This is what my family's like. They didn't come here for me. They came here because of you. I think, given your situation, my mother's adopted you. She wants you to know that you're not alone."

Keith had no idea what to say to that, so he remained silent.

He maintained the same silence throughout the service, struggling hard against the unexpected waves of emotion that inexplicably beat against the beaches of his soul, wearing him down.

As the service was winding down, just when Keith thought his ordeal was finally coming to a close, the priest performing the service looked out on the rows of people he had been addressing.

"And now," the priest said, his deep, gentle voice going out to the very last pew, "if anyone here would like to add his or her own words to this service, please feel free to come up and say something about Mrs. O'Connell. Remember, it doesn't have to be polished. It just has to be from the heart. I'm sure that Dorothy would be very pleased."

A reluctance to be the first to speak kept people in their seats initially.

The priest looked around at the upturned faces, appearing to be searching for not just someone, but someone in particular.

And then his gaze honed in on Keith.

"Mr. O'Connell?" he called out, his tone meant to coax Dorothy's son out of his seat.

Keith began to move his head from side to side, wanting more than anything to be excused. If all else failed, he was going to point to his throat and just shake his head, begging off by means of a lie.

But Kenzie whispered into his ear, "Just say something about how you'll miss her sunny disposition and be done with it. If you don't, you'll always feel like there was some unfinished business left in the wake of her demise."

He kept his voice down, insisting, "I can't go up there and lie, gushing about how I'm going to miss the sound of her voice."

"Then don't lie," she countered. "Just pick your truths.

You have to do this. You've come this far," she reminded him. "You can't just fold at the eleventh hour."

What he wanted to do was tell her that yes, he could. But he knew she was right. If he didn't do this, everyone would know there had been ill feelings between his mother and him. There were, but it was no one's business but his.

So, although it went against everything he thought was right, Keith slowly rose to his feet and began to walk up to the pulpit.

## Chapter Thirteen

Keith curled his fingers around either side of the pulpit, gripping it. He still wasn't sure how he had managed to make his way from the pew to the place vacated by the man who had been his mother's priest for the last thirty-one years. He couldn't remember putting one foot in front of the other.

His mouth felt like cotton and his mind was as close to empty as it had ever been.

What the hell was he doing up here?

He should never have gotten up, never allowed Kenzie to urge him on with that look of hers.

Now he was trapped up here.

His eyes shifted to the first pew. To Kenzie. She was smiling at him, her eyes urging him on.

Encouraging him.

And suddenly, just like that, his mind came alive.

"Looking around this church, I can see that my mother had a lot of friends. A lot of people are going to miss her now that she's gone. Since people are all different in the way they react to things, everyone will undoubtedly miss something else about my mother."

He could almost hear Kenzie cheering him on, like a mother watching her child take his first wobbly steps. He should have been resentful, he told himself.

For some odd reason, he wasn't.

"Me, I'll miss the mother I once knew. The one who stayed up late, putting the finishing touches on two dinosaur costumes so that my sister, Amy, and I wouldn't miss out on going trick-or-treating the next day. She stayed up late sewing, even though she had put in a full day's work and had to go in early the next morning to her second job. She worked two jobs because that's what it took to feed and clothe us."

He paused for a moment, reining in emotions that threatened to break free. It took him a couple more minutes before he could continue.

"I'll miss the mother who worked hard to help me memorize words for my spelling test so I could finally ace my retest instead of flunking it the way I'd been doing—spelling was never my strong suit," he added in an aside that had some in the church laughing in commiseration. "When I complained that I was too dumb to remember how to spell the words, she got angry with me and insisted that I wasn't. She got angry because I had run myself down and she didn't believe in doing that. Positive reinforcement was her thing."

He paused as his throat tightened. "I'll miss the mother who wouldn't quit, who refused to give up, even when things seemed hopeless." He took a breath before pushing on. "She lost her way after Amy died. I wish I could have helped her find it again, the way she used to help me find mine. I'll…" He pressed his lips together, feeling naked and exposed. "I'll miss my mother," he concluded in a quiet voice, and then stepped down.

He didn't remember taking his seat again, didn't remember actually even sitting down, either. And he was only vaguely aware that someone took his hand, threaded her fingers through his and lightly squeezed, conveying so many unspoken sentiments of comfort with that simple gesture.

Slowly, by degrees, as another voice began to speak from the pulpit about his mother, he became aware of Kenzie. Aware that it was her hand that had taken his, aware that she had been the one to squeeze it. Her eyes when they met his were filled not with pity but with sympathy.

Sympathy and tears.

"You did good," she whispered to him.

He couldn't answer her. He was afraid that his voice would break if he did. It bothered him that he could feel this way even after he had built up this tall wall around himself. The wall that was supposed to keep his feelings about his mother at bay and contained at all times.

He'd been keeping the wall in place for so long, he'd been certain that he had no feelings left, not for his mother, not for anyone. And yet there they were. Feelings. Feelings just waiting to ambush him. To prick him and make him bleed.

"I shouldn't have come," he told Kenzie when he could finally trust his voice not to break. The service had ended, and a church full of people had dutifully filed out and into their separate vehicles. They were all headed for the same place.

The cemetery.

The drive was a very short one, practically over before it began.

Kenzie remained steadfast. "You would have never forgiven yourself if you hadn't," she told him as they climbed out of the somber black sedan.

They fell into step, joining the flow of people heading toward the area of All Saints Cemetery that had just been prepared for the latest burial ceremony. It was to be his mother's final resting place.

Or at least where his mother's casket was going into the ground, he thought cynically. The dead didn't rest. They didn't do anything anymore.

"Not exactly thrilled with myself right now," he finally responded. He'd paused for so long, she thought he either hadn't heard her or, more likely, had chosen to ignore her.

"You can get through this," she told him with the conviction of someone who had utter faith in what she was saying. She was doing her best to convey that to him. "Just keep putting one foot in front of the other the way you've been doing."

What he wanted to do was put one foot in front of the other in the opposite direction and get as far away from the service—and her—as he could. For entirely different reasons. But he knew he couldn't, not without calling a great deal of attention to himself, which was the *last* thing he wanted to do.

So he made his way with the others to his mother's gravesite, acutely aware that Kenzie was right at his side every step of the way. Kenzie and that family of hers who seemed to insist on being there as a complete set—just the way they had been at the church.

He wanted to send her away, to send her whole family away. Yet in a strange way he couldn't begin to explain, he was grateful for their presence.

He sensed that they just wanted to be supportive for no other reason than, as Kenzie had said, he needed them to be.

He had to admit they were exceptional people. Just like she was.

Keith squared his shoulders and stood at the gravesite as the priest spoke words about his mother and her life that he barely heard. After a few minutes, it all became one continuous buzzing.

And then the casket was lowered and people were dropping roses onto it.

Where had all those roses come from? he wondered absently. This was winter, the third week in December. Weren't flowers meant for the spring?

He looked at Kenzie, and he had his answer. As with everything else, she must have taken care of this detail for him. She'd had the roses brought to the gravesite and distributed among the mourners.

She was always one step ahead. Certainly one step ahead of him.

"It's over," Kenzie whispered to him as the gathering at the gravesite began to break up. Taking his hand, she lightly tugged on it, indicating the direction he needed to take.

Because he suddenly felt drained, he let her lead, quietly following her out of the cemetery to the vehicle that stood waiting for them.

"You're doing very well," Kenzie said, her voice breaking into the endless silence riding with them in the vehicle.

"Don't patronize me," he told her tersely. Keith knew he had to come off like an angry, wounded bear. It was either that or break down. This was turning out to be a lot harder on him than he had anticipated.

"I'm not." The answer was neither defensive nor cloying. It was a simple matter-of-fact statement. "But you do still have an attitude problem," she pointed out. "People are just trying to be sympathetic, nothing more. Take it at face value and be gracious."

He swallowed the first words that rose to his lips. No matter what he felt, she didn't deserve to be shouted at. He let out a deep breath. It didn't help. His nerves felt frayed.

"Do I really have to go to the reception?" He knew the answer to that, but there was a part of him that was still hoping for a reprieve.

Kenzie merely looked at him. "It's being held at the house."

"That still doesn't answer my question," he told her, knowing he was being irrational, but still unable to refrain.

"Okay, then I'll answer it," she told him gamely as the driver entered Keith's development. "Yes, you need to go to the reception."

"Why? I said my piece at the funeral service. I attended the burial at the cemetery. The reception is just people milling around, talking over food."

"Well, you can talk, and you do eat. Shouldn't be a problem," she told him practically. And then she squeezed his hand. There was that silent encouragement again, he couldn't help thinking. But he didn't pull his hand away. "Just one more hurdle and then you can go back to being Mr. Congeniality and winning everyone over with your happy patter."

"Sarcasm?" He raised his eyebrow as if taking offense. "I just came back from the cemetery."

"That's why I toned it down," she told him, a wide, guileless smile on her lips.

He had no idea why he found that heartening—but he did.

The next few hours were a blur of people shaking his hand, offering words of condolence and relating stories he told himself he had no interest in hearing. Stories that convinced him in the last years of her life, his mother had cared for other people—any people—more than she had for him.

The sting of the angry words that marked their last encounter kept coming back to him over the course of the afternoon and evening, leaving a bitter taste in his mouth and an ache in his chest.

Just when he didn't think he could take much more, to his surprise the woman that Kenzie had hired to do the catering for the reception—a Mrs. Manetti, he thought she'd told him—came to his rescue by quietly telling the people that the reception would be closing down shortly.

After that, guests began taking their leave, pausing to say a few final words to him before going out the door.

And then, finally, the last of the guests were gone.

"That woman certainly knows how to clear a room," he commented to Kenzie, savoring the relief he was feeling.

Kenzie smiled as she nodded, watching the caterer preside over the room's cleanup. "Mrs. Manetti is good at reading people."

"I don't follow," he told Kenzie.

"I think she realized that you were reaching the end of your rope, and she could tell there was just so much more you could put up with. She probably said what she did so you could have some peace and quiet, let everything that transpired today settle and gel." She looked at him for a long, scrutinizing moment, then observed, "Apparently she was right. I think you're just about smiled out."

Well, she certainly had that right, Keith thought. The muscles of his face felt as if they were in danger of cramping up if he had to spend another five minutes smiling at well-intentioned strangers telling him what they deemed to be amusing stories about his mother.

Kenzie patted his face. "A really hot shower might help relax that."

"Yeah," he murmured, looking around the living room. It had emptied even faster than he had anticipated.

And as for Mrs. Manetti's crew, they were exceptionally efficient. The trays of food and beverages, both hard and soft, had been whisked away, and the extraneous plates and glasses that had littered the family room and living room were gone as if they had never existed.

Everything had been washed and put away in what amounted to a blink of an eye.

"It seems almost a little empty in comparison to earlier," Keith couldn't help commenting.

"It seems a *lot* empty," Kenzie corrected him with a laugh.

The next moment, she realized that just might be the trouble. As much as Keith had seemed as if he wanted to be alone, now she was hearing something else in his voice. There was almost a loneliness that she hadn't picked up on earlier.

"Listen, I don't really have anywhere to be—just some last minute presents waiting to be wrapped, but nothing that can't wait," she told him. "I can stay here for a while, keep you company."

Keith frowned slightly. He still didn't want any pity from her no matter how good she'd been about everything. "I don't need a babysitter."

"And I don't recall offering to be one," she told him matter-of-factly. "I do, however, remember offering to spend a little time with my friend." The television monitor, tucked within an entertainment unit over in the corner, caught her eye. "Maybe watch an old movie over some popcorn."

"What old movie?" he asked.

Her shoulders rose and fell gamely. She was secretly congratulating herself on getting him to open to the proposition. "You pick."

It didn't matter to him—with one exception. "I don't want to watch some sentimental tear-jerker."

"That's good, because neither do I." She didn't want him watching something weepy. He needed an upbeat movie, preferably a good comedy. "We can stream a movie—or simpler still, just channel surf."

She had a feeling it really wasn't about what was on the screen for him. As long as there was something flickering across it, making sufficient background noise, that just might be enough. She was hoping they'd wind up talking through it. He needed to talk.

"Why are you doing all this?" he asked out of the blue as she turned on the monitor. "Why are you handling everything for me, going these extra miles, being my buffer, my go-between?"

"That's simple enough to answer," she deadpanned. "I have this Girl Scout merit badge that I'm trying to earn." Kenzie struggled to keep a hint of a smile from curving the corners of her mouth.

"Seriously," Keith insisted.

She raised her eyebrows in feigned surprise. "You mean I'm *not* earning a Girl Scout merit badge for this? Bummer."

"Kenzie, why are you doing this?" he repeated, enunciated each word slowly and firmly.

She stopped teasing. "Because you're my friend. Because you're hurting. Because as a kid, I used to bring home stray puppies and feed them." She shrugged, as if she had no real say in the direction her behavior took. "It's a tough habit to break."

"So is making up stories and spitting out wisecracks," he observed wryly.

"No argument," Kenzie acknowledged. "But I don't know anyone like that." Sitting down on the sofa, she looked around the immediate area. "Where's your remote hiding?"

Keith nodded toward the other side of the coffee table. They both reached for it at the same time. And wound up grabbing opposite ends of the remote simultaneously.

Keith automatically pulled the remote—and because of that, her—to him before Kenzie could think to let it go. Unprepared for the sudden move, Kenzie lost her balance and wound up bumping up against his chest.

It was hard to say which of them was more startled by the very abrupt, sudden contact.

Surprise gave way to something far more basic.

Before he could stop himself, Keith cupped her face with his hands. The next moment, he brought his mouth down to hers.

Moved, emotional against his will, Keith kissed her to express his gratitude, to in effect say things that he couldn't find the right words to articulate.

He kissed her because it was the fastest and the simplest way to express himself and to make her realize that he was very aware just how much she had put herself out for him.

He meant to kiss her and just leave it at that.

But the kiss didn't wind up ending anything. Instead, it began something. By its very nature, it wound up opening up a whole volume of feelings he hadn't even been vaguely aware were there.

One kiss grew into another.

And another.

Each kiss was feeding upon the last and gaining in depth and breadth until they threatened to engulf not just him, but Kenzie, as well.

This was, a voice in his head whispered, the point of no return. This was where he stopped, took a breath and stepped back.

*Move!*

But none of that was happening.

The kiss was multiplying, mushrooming, demanding more and more from him. It was creating hopes and expectations that he was so very tempted to grasp hold of—and hold on to for dear life.

In her conscious mind, Kenzie knew this wasn't really Keith. It wasn't the man she had come to know or even the teenager she'd had such a huge crush on all those years ago.

Grief was making Keith act in a way he wouldn't if his soul hadn't fallen into some deep, dark abyss of hopelessness from which there was no return.

But there was *always* a way to return, Kenzie's mind argued. She had to let him know that so he wouldn't somehow wind up doing something he was going to regret deeply the moment he was thinking clearly again.

Any second now, she was going to pull her head back and make the wrong comment. The last thing she wanted was something to leave him feeling worse than before.

But how could this wondrous thing she was feeling be bad? something inside her argued.

Right now, it felt as if she was on fire. And the fire was good.

Better than good.

This was exactly what she'd always felt it would be like, kissing Keith.

Heaven in bright, neon lights.

## Chapter Fourteen

There was liquid heat going through her veins. The word *more* echoed over and over in her head, obliterating any lingering thoughts of resistance.

Kenzie gave up even the slightest ghost of a protest, letting it disintegrate into nothingness. Melting as quickly as she was in the flame of his kiss.

*Finally!*

Her heart hammered wildly, joyfully embracing the feeling. After all this time, she was finally going to discover what it was like to make love with the man she'd once been so completely convinced was her soul mate.

The man she realized she'd always been in love with.

Keith had gone on to college, then left Bedford and Southern California altogether in the year after Amy had died, and she'd made her peace with that. Life for her had continued. She'd even tried her hand at a couple of semiserious relationships, but nothing ever took. There had never been anyone to fill her thoughts and dreams the way that Keith once had, never anyone whom she'd even come close to regarding as her soul mate.

No one she really wanted to spend the rest of her life with. That was because the position had always remained filled. Keith was the only man who qualified for that title—soul mate—then and now.

The very first time his lips had touched hers, she knew with certainty there was no point in really fighting her reaction to him, in pretending it was wrong, or happening for the wrong reasons.

No matter what tomorrow brought—and she was a big girl now—she didn't expect Keith to have some sort of a life-changing epiphany when dawn came. Didn't expect him to sweep her off her feet, declare he'd been blind up to this moment and he wanted to uproot his life, move back here and spend the rest of his days loving her just the way he was tonight.

Granted, it would have been wonderful…

But she was well aware that this wasn't some splashy 1940s big studio movie. This was life and infinitely more real than any so-called reality show. She knew not to expect anything more than what was happening at this very moment.

And what was happening this very moment was beyond words.

Beyond wonderful.

Everywhere Keith kissed her, everywhere he touched her, she felt the area quickening and coming vibrantly alive. She felt absolutely radiant with such a spectrum of feelings, of reactions, that it would have exhausted her to try to describe exactly what it was that she was experiencing, even to herself.

So she didn't even try.

She instead savored the overwhelming sensations. She

gave herself permission to squeeze every last drop out of what was happening, to soar beyond the highest pinnacle as sensation built on sensation within her body.

The second her skin ignited in response to Keith's hands, Kenzie eagerly tore away the physical barriers that existed between them. Starting with Keith's shirt, she worked her way down to the very last shred of clothing he had on.

It occurred to her only belatedly that she was pulling his clothing away from his body at the very same time that he was undressing hers.

And then there were no barriers, physical or otherwise.

Their bodies came together as if their very souls were magnetized, compelled to pull each other in.

She was his for the taking.

Keith had no idea what came over him. This had never happened to him before, not anywhere to this degree. Even when he was an adolescent doing his best to navigate through a sea of raging hormones, he had never felt like this, never experienced this all-encompassing need to make love the way he did right at this moment with Kenzie.

He told himself it was the grief fogging up his thinking, throwing him off balance. But he knew it was more than that. He wasn't just stumbling about, blindly feeling his way around. He wasn't blind. He could see with complete clarity.

And what he saw was Kenzie.

Nothing else but Kenzie.

She was his focus, his beacon, his guiding light—and she was drawing him in. Bringing him in to what could very well be his destiny.

It was completely irrational, but he felt as if he couldn't

continue existing in any manner, shape or form if he couldn't have Kenzie, if he couldn't make love with her tonight.

*Now.*

Struggling not to behave like some sort of deranged madman or rutting animal, Keith struggled to exercise supreme control over himself and move with patient restraint, not devour but savor the taste of her mouth, the feel of her body as his hands glided over her silken skin.

He had no idea what tomorrow would bring, and he was torn between the plans he'd set in stone—leaving here and never looking back—and the very new, formless, undefined feelings he was experiencing right at this moment.

Feelings, he realized, that had begun to take root from the very moment she had walked into his life again.

There was no denying, even as he continued making love to every inch of her body, that he was the very epitome of confusion and indecision. He, who had always tread so confidently, so clear-eyed through every step of his life, found himself stumbling now.

He couldn't think beyond the moment, certainly not about anything that lay on the horizon. All he could think about was now—that he had to have her now—because there could very well be no later.

Like a man who sensed he was dying at dawn, he made love with Kenzie as if he'd never get another opportunity to do so. Perhaps never even see her again after tonight.

Desperation created a passion of unimaginable proportions.

He made love with her as if he was on fire, made love to each and every part of her before he finally succumbed and, unable to hold himself back for even another tenth of a second—made love to *all* of her.

* * *

Her heart was pounding so hard, she was having trouble catching her breath. He was making her absolutely, deliciously crazy.

She arched her body toward each wonderful, cascading sensation as it first exploded within her, then fanned out into a countless myriad of lights.

She had no idea it was possible or how he managed to do it, but Keith was creating climax after climax within her. He brought her up and over so many times that she was convinced, as she finally lay there all but panting from sheer, thrilling exhaustion, that she had died and hadn't become completely aware of it.

The ecstasy she was experiencing launched her into a semiconscious, euphoric state.

Kenzie clung to it as if it were her life preserver.

While she didn't want to relinquish her hold on what was tantalizingly echoing through her body, she didn't think she could take more pleasure.

She almost giggled then because it was obvious, from the urgent way Keith was kissing her, that she would have to readjust her perceived and preconceived notions about her own limits.

Her capacity for pleasure was just going to have to increase—and *fast*.

Because he was ramping up the parameters.

With her last ounce of strength, Kenzie raised herself up on her elbows and captured his lips first, beginning a new and final round to the lovemaking that had begun so suddenly a luscious eternity ago.

Her taking the initiative almost made him crazy, instantly increasing the desire he felt, spiking it in his veins even as it all but brought him to his knees.

He deepened the kiss between them, then went on to

spread kisses along her body as she twisted and turned beneath his mouth. Every single part of her eagerly sought to be touched by his lips, anointed by his tongue. Each contact had her racing heart singing.

She wanted him.

Wanted him down to her very core, and she didn't know how much longer she could hold out. Her body was all but literally crying out for his.

"Make love with me now," Kenzie said hoarsely. It was half a command, half a plea.

There was no way he could resist even a second longer. Her entreaty broke the very last band of control he had left.

Keith threaded his fingers through hers, felt her body arching up to press against his. She urged him on to the final union.

Even if his very life had depended on it, he couldn't have held back for a heartbeat longer. His body positioned over hers, Keith drove himself into her with as much power as he had left in his diminished arsenal.

The moment they were joined, a growing rhythm overtook them, dictating their final moments.

The tempo increased, urging them on faster and faster until they were all but racing toward the all-encompassing explosion, the culmination of everything that had come before.

And when they reached the top of the summit, tightly holding on to one another, the explosion shook their bodies, then rained down an exhilarating tranquility on them that was equal parts joy, euphoria and then delicious exhaustion.

After the ecstasy retreated into a warm feeling of well-being, Keith held her to him in a way he had never held anything before. Gently, tenderly, but with an underlying urgency, because he feared that the second he let go of her, everything—she, the feeling, *everything*—would just vanish as if it had never really existed.

So he held her until they both finally drifted off to sleep, each willing dawn to remain a thousand miles away.

But dawn came, the way it always had, the way it always would. It came and nudged aside the darkness, bringing with it the morning light.

Keith opened his eyes, more than a little surprised to find himself still here, in the family room of the house he had grown up in.

His mother's house.

The realization drove the last remnants of sleep away from him as if sleep had been a figment of his imagination,

He almost sat up then. Except that he couldn't. His mouth curved.

There was a woman with her head on his chest, and he couldn't sit up without disturbing her. If he disturbed her, it would probably wake her up.

So he lay there, his arms now lightly instead of tightly folded around her.

Feeling her breathe soothed him. He needed soothing right about now. A great deal had happened last night. He had a lot to think about. But he didn't want to think about anything.

He wanted the world to go away and this moment to be frozen in time so that nothing changed and this brand-new, wondrous feeling he was trying so desperately to hang on to would remain forever—or at the very least, last a little while longer.

That was all he wanted, just a little while longer— since eternity was apparently out of the question and off the table.

God, he was rambling on even in his own head.

At least he hadn't opened his mouth to let any of this out. He sought some sort of rational order he could easily slip everything that had happened into.

*Good luck with that*, he mocked himself.

Kenzie was stirring.

He froze.

Her hair was tickling his face. What could he say to her? *Should* he say anything to her, or just pretend to be asleep?

He opted for door number two—but it was too late. She'd picked up her head and was looking straight at him, so there was no use in pretending he was asleep.

Resigned, he murmured, "'Morning."

"Yes," Kenzie agreed, stretching like a cat against him and sending his temperature—not to mention his heart—soaring. "It is that." Her mouth curved, amused. Kenzie looked into his eyes, her smile growing wider. "You're still here. Is that a good sign?"

Evasiveness had become a habit. He sank into it naturally. "You were asleep on my chest. I couldn't leave."

"Ah, so it's just a sign, not a good one. You're here because you're too much of a gentleman to push me aside in order to make your getaway." She pretended to mull it over, then nodded. "Not as romantic as I would have hoped, but I'll take it."

"Um, Kenzie—" His voice faltered slightly. He had no idea what to say next, or at least how to phrase what he wanted to say next. Making love with her had entirely taken away his edge.

"Relax," Kenzie laughed, lovingly touching his cheek. "I'm just kidding. There's no reason for you to turn so pale."

"I didn't turn pale," he protested.

Kenzie rolled her eyes. "Oh, puh-lease. In comparison, you'd make a ghost look like he had a suntan." She laughed and the sound was oddly comforting. Even though he thought it was at his expense. "It's okay, Keith. Breathe." She touched his cheek again, as if that would somehow help calm him down. "We made love and it was beyond wonderful—at least for me. But I'm not expecting to hear our banns being announced at mass, and I'm not about to drag you off to look at wedding rings," she assured him, her eyes dancing with humor.

"We made love last night, but today is a new day, with new problems, new hurdles to leap over. If I'm not mistaken, it's the first day the house is going to be open to the public in hopes of enchanting them. So unless you're game to bring a whole new meaning to the term 'unwrapped presents under the Christmas tree,' I suggest we get up from under the tree, get dressed and clean the family room."

He blinked, trying to absorb her words. The woman talked faster than anyone he had ever known, and that included lawyers. "Then last night didn't mean anything to you?"

How could he possibly say that? she couldn't help wondering.

Maybe it was breaking some kind of unspoken law about admitting far too much, but she told him, "It meant *everything* to me. But it wasn't a proposal and I'm not about to demand one. So, like I said, let's get cracking and whip this house back into shape."

Gratitude overwhelmed him. Before he could think to stop himself, he went with instinct. Keith spun her around to face him and kissed her.

Kissed her long and hard with mounting feeling.

When she finally got herself to pull back, Kenzie drew

in a deep, deep breath and shook her head. The man definitely didn't understand the concept of a temporary retreat for the sake of getting things that needed doing done.

"You do that again and I'm not going to be responsible for what happens next. There's just so much self-control a woman should be expected to exercise, especially when confronted with a lover who's so incredibly hot," she told him with a wink.

And with that, Kenzie quickly put distance between them before all her good intentions went flying out the window and she threw herself into his arms.

## Chapter Fifteen

"The tree is a very nice touch," Maizie said with warm approval later that morning. The words were addressed to Keith. True to her word, the lively agent had arrived early to make sure there were no last-minute hiccups she needed to smooth out before the open house got underway at one. "Glad to see you decided to take my advice. It really creates a family-friendly atmosphere."

Keith never believed in taking credit that didn't belong to him. Working in a law firm had taught him that doing so could bite him later. Besides, he wanted Kenzie to have her due.

"Actually, it was Kenzie who insisted on it," he said, nodding in Kenzie's direction.

Maizie looked toward the younger woman. If anything, the agent's smile just grew deeper.

"Well, she was right. This really makes it feel less like just another house on the market and more like a home. Unless they're looking strictly for investment purposes, prospective buyers react very positively to that sort of thing. They like knowing the house they're considering buying lends itself well to a family scenario." Maizie made her way from the family room to the kitchen. "Have you been staying here?" she asked him.

His first impulse was to deny it. But something told him the savvy little woman would somehow know he was lying. So he told her the truth.

"I wasn't going to, but—"

Keith abruptly stopped himself from explaining any further. There was no need for any confessions. This woman was his agent, and while she was an exceptionally nice, warm, intelligent woman, she was definitely not his priest.

Less than a month ago, he wouldn't have felt the need to say anything at all. Just what was going on with him? Keith silently demanded.

"Yes, I am," he finally admitted. "Why?"

"No reason," Maizie told him with a careless shrug that could have been interpreted in so many ways. "It's just that the house appears to be exceptionally neat." She turned a warm smile on him. "Someone raised you well."

He bit his tongue, swallowing the first answer that rose to his lips. The answer rejecting the idea that he'd been raised well at all. But if he were being totally honest, he would admit that he *had* been raised well. It was only in the aftermath of those years that everything fell to pieces.

"Yes, well, I thought the house wouldn't exactly show very well and attract buyers if it was a mess."

Maizie inclined her head, her eyes shining with humor. "Very true."

Finished looking around, Maizie set down the flyers she'd had run off on the coffee table in plain view of the entrance. The handouts enumerated the home's best features as well as its upgrades.

She turned to Keith. "Well, I hope you have somewhere to go today between one and five." Then, in case the reason for that was eluding him—this was, as far as she knew, his first time as a seller—Maizie told him, "It's customary not to have the home owner around during an open house. Makes it less awkward for everyone."

He hadn't actually thought about that since, initially, he hadn't planned even to be in town at this point. "Um, sure, I…"

"I'm taking him to my store so he can see where some of his family's items will be going until someone snaps them up and gives them a good home," Kenzie informed the agent cheerfully.

Maizie looked from Kenzie to her client. "Judging from his bewildered expression, I think you forgot to tell him about that, dear."

That was because she'd just thought of it, Kenzie silently answered. Ever the subtle saleswoman, she proceeded to sell Keith on the idea.

"It'll be interesting," she assured him. "And maybe you'll see something there you might want to buy to give someone as a Christmas present."

"Why would I want to do that?"

His answer made it sound as if…

"Wait, you don't give Christmas presents?" Kenzie stared at him, stunned. "To anyone?" she asked incredulously. "Not even to those senior law partners you work for?"

He looked at her with surprise. "That would just be a form of bribery. They wouldn't stand for it."

Kenzie blew out a breath. She had no idea that the situation was this bad. Keith's soul really needed rescuing.

Apparently of like mind with Kenzie, the look on Maizie's face was nothing if not sympathetic.

"I'd say you had your work cut out for you, dear," the older woman said before she left the room, saying she was retrieving her business cards from the trunk of her car.

Kenzie, meanwhile, was still frozen in place. "You were kidding, weren't you? About not giving any Christmas presents?" There was more than a hint of a hopeful note in her voice.

Keith shrugged off her question, telling himself that her obvious disappointment shouldn't have bothered him.

*Why* was it bothering him? he silently demanded.

"Don't have anyone to give them to."

It was, in a nutshell, his go-to excuse for not participating in the holidays. With Amy gone and his mother heretofore inaccessible, Christmas and the trappings that went with it ceased to have any meaning to him.

This, Kenzie decided, would require drastic measures.

And then a possible solution occurred to her.

"I have a better place to take you than my shop," she announced suddenly. "Just give me a few minutes to make a call."

It was getting so that he could almost read her mind. At least he could this time around. "I don't know what you think you need to do for me, but I assure you I do not need any—"

"Yeah, you do," she said, cutting him off. "Don't worry," she added, "It'll be painless."

And then she stopped talking because whoever she had just dialed on her cell phone had obviously picked up. Rather than continue her dialogue with Keith, Kenzie held up her finger in a silent instruction to stop his words midflow.

Kenzie turned away so he wouldn't overhear her. The

move was done out of habit, but he had to admit that his curiosity had been piqued—and his impatience was fueled. He didn't need whatever holiday sleight-of-hand Kenzie thought she was going to perform.

With that in mind, since she wasn't facing him, he decided he'd leave the house while she was talking. Slipping out the front door—the agent had already gone back inside and was doing something in one of the rooms—Keith came within a foot of making good his getaway.

Kenzie caught up to him just as he was about to get into his car. He'd opened the door and was going to slide in behind the steering wheel when he felt her hand on his shoulder.

"You're coming with me," she announced as if she didn't realize she had foiled his getaway.

He turned around to face her, impatience swaddling each word. "Kenzie, I don't need a babysitter."

"Good," she countered, "because no one's offering to babysit you." The significance of the words he'd chosen suddenly hit her. "If anything, you will be the one doing the sitting."

She'd totally lost him with that. "Come again?"

But Kenzie didn't go into any more detailed explanations. All she said was a very pregnant, "You'll see."

Keith could only think of one logical scenario as she commandeered the keys from him and told him to get into the passenger's seat. "Are you kidnapping me to a motel room?" The situation as he painted it was not without its rather large merits.

Starting the car, she pulled out of the driveway. "Well, you're half right."

"Which half?"

Kenzie spared him a glance as she took a right turn at the next through street. "I'm kidnapping you."

"Not to a motel room?" To anyone listening, it sounded as if Keith was kidding. He wasn't, at least not entirely.

Kenzie pretended to roll the thought over in her mind. "Maybe later. As a reward," she added.

"For me?" he questioned.

Even with her facing forward, he could see how deep her smile went. "For both of us."

Keith laughed, shaking his head. The woman was nothing if not unique. "Now you really have me curious."

"Good," she declared. To his frustration and surprise, she made no effort to explain anything further.

Keith tried another approach to unravel what she was up to. "Can I ask who you called?"

Kenzie inclined her head in a careless fashion. "You can ask."

It didn't take a philosopher to understand what she was saying. "But you won't tell me."

"I won't tell you," she confirmed, adding, "I figure it's more interesting for you if I just keep you guessing."

That sounded too much like a game, and he needed to let her know something right off the top. "Look, I'm not into playing games."

"Too bad." She sounded as if she genuinely meant that. "It actually might come in handy. Maybe it'll come back to you after a while."

"What the hell are you talking about?" Keith demanded, feeling as if he'd somehow gotten all tangled up and was sinking.

"Christmas, Keith. I'm talking about Christmas."

She wasn't going to tell him anything, he concluded. Since he was here, Keith decided that he might as well just let this all play itself out. Maybe there would finally be answers when she got to wherever it was she was going.

Sliding back in his seat, Keith pushed it into a resting position. "If you say so."

Kenzie laughed then and reached over to pat his arm, keeping her eyes on the road. "Not too far now," she promised.

As far as he was concerned, it had already gone way too far.

"We're here," she announced a little more than ten minutes later.

"Here?" Keith repeated, looking around. "Exactly where's 'here'?" he asked.

As far as he could make out, she had just turned onto a gravel-strewn parking lot. After driving only a few feet more, she came to a stop in front of a long, single-story building that was badly in need of paint not to mention some very crucially missing stucco work.

There was a sign across the front of the building, but the sun was in his eyes, so he couldn't make it out.

But Kenzie wasn't listening to him as she got out of the car. Instead, she seemed to be looking around for something.

Or someone, as it turned out.

The second she spotted who she was looking for, she broke into a wreath of smiles. A moment later, Kenzie's mystery person had joined them.

"You made it," Kenzie cried in relief.

Almost reluctantly, Keith got out of the car to see who she was talking to.

The next second, his mouth dropped open.

"Mrs. Bradshaw, I didn't expect to see you here," he said to the slender woman in gray slacks, a pink sweater and a matching hoodie.

"I have a habit of popping up in odd places," Kenzie's mother conceded. "Hello, dear." Andrea paused to greet

him with a quick kiss against his cheek, treating him as
if he were her son instead of just her daughter's…what?
Her daughter's what? Keith silently demanded of himself.

He really hadn't figured out what to call their relationship—or if it actually *was* a relationship.

Turning toward her daughter, Andrea went on to tell
her, "I brought everything, just the way you asked me to."

"Everything?" Keith echoed.

He was beginning to feel like a parrot, repeating words
that became no clearer to him the second time around.

Taking pity on him, Kenzie turned toward him and
said, "She means toys."

"Toys?" He was no more enlightened now than he had
been a moment ago.

Kenzie pressed her lips together to keep from laughing at him. "All right, you'll have to learn how to speak
in full sentences if you're going to help me."

"Help you with what?" Keith demanded. He was down
that rabbit hole again, he thought irritably. And she wasn't
helping. He was beginning to think she was enjoying his
confusion.

"Better," Kenzie said, nodding her approval. "But still
needs a little work."

In mounting desperation, he turned toward her mother.
"What is she talking about?"

"I'm never quite sure, Keith," Andrea admitted, com-
miserating with him. "But I've learned that if you hang
in there long enough, it eventually all makes sense after
a bit."

"No big mystery," Kenzie told him, sounding, to his
way of thinking, just a little too innocent as she added,
"I'm playing Santa Claus, and you're my helper."

Keith realized her mother was in on this little scenario,
as well, when Andrea said to her, "Really, dear, I don't

want to be stereotypical about this, but since Santa was a man, don't you think Keith should play Santa Claus and *you* should be *his* helper?"

Kenzie pretended that lightning had suddenly struck, clearing everything up.

"You know, that might make more sense, after all. You can be Santa Claus," she told him. And just to make it official, she produced a Santa suit, complete with a red cap from a bag that her mother handed her. She slipped the hat snugly on Keith's head. "There, it's official. I hereby dub you Santa Claus for a day! Now let's go get you into this getup so you can start making some very deserving little kids happy."

After five minutes and one detour into the kitchen so he could put on the suit, Keith stood frowning at the traditional costume that hung around his body. He'd been forced to put it on over his own clothes in an attempt to deal with its size, but it was still dangerously baggy and threatening to fall off at any moment.

"I really don't think I can do this," he told Kenzie as she fussed around him, using safety pins to decrease the size where she could.

"It would have been even looser on me," she told him, adding, "We have to work with what we have."

"No, we don't. *I* don't," he corrected her.

Kenzie stopped what she was doing, one last safety pin still in her hand. She didn't look at him with exasperation or annoyance. Instead, she searched her mind for a way to approach him logically instead of using emotions to win him over.

"Have you ever pleaded one of your cases before a judge?" she asked him quietly.

Was she kidding? He wasn't a law clerk. He was an accredited *lawyer*. "Yes, of course I have."

Nodding, Kenzie continued. "Was he a friendly judge?"

Subsequent judges had melded together, but not his first one. That man's dour face was still as vividly clear in his mind as if the trial had taken place yesterday. "Not particularly," he answered gruffly.

"Then I guess, since you didn't think it was a slam-dunk, you gave up." She said it as if it was a foregone conclusion.

"No, of course not."

"But you didn't win."

He saw where Kenzie was going with this. "Yes, I won."

Kenzie smiled, her argument made. "Then you can do this," she assured Keith with total confidence. "These kids are more than willing to meet you halfway. Having Santa Claus find them brings hope into their young lives. And the gifts in here," she told him, patting the side of the large sagging red sack, made out of the same material that his suit was, "will sell themselves. All you have to do is say 'Ho-ho-ho' and the toys in the bag will do the rest of your talking for you." She put on the finishing touch: pulling a white beard out of the same bag that had held his costume. After helping him put it on, she looked at him and grinned. "Hottest looking Santa I've ever seen, bar none. Ready?"

Keith was still not completely convinced he could pull this off. "No, I don't think I'm—"

He didn't get a chance to finish because she suddenly sang out, "Showtime!" grabbed hold of his hand and pulled him from the safety of the kitchen into the pure nerve-racking atmosphere of the homeless shelter's common room, where the parents and children spent time getting to know one another and hopefully made connections that would last them a lifetime. Or, at the very least, help get their minds off their situations for a little while.

"I sure hope you know what I'm doing," Keith said, eyeing the group of children he saw at the far end of the room.

"Absolutely. Bringing hope," she told him, looking pointedly at him.

He wasn't ready for this. Wasn't ready to interact with small, thin faces, all eagerly hoping that Santa had remembered them.

But ready or not, here they came, he thought as a group of children suddenly and enthusiastically surrounded him.

"What's in your bag, Mr. Santa?" one little blonde girl, who couldn't have been any older than six, asked as she tugged on Keith's sleeve.

For a split second, she reminded him of Amy when she had been that small. The same hair color, the same delicate bone structure.

And suddenly, it wasn't so hard playing Santa Claus any more. "Why don't we open it and see?" Keith answered, adding, "Who knows? There might even be something here for you."

"Really?" the little girl asked, her bright blue eyes growing to the size of the proverbial saucers as she turned them to the large bag Keith had managed to bring into the room.

"Really," Keith replied.

He pulled back the straining sides of the red bag and took out the first wrapped package. He pretended to examine it, shaking it slightly. And then he saw the lettering, ever so faint, across the front.

The word was Girl, telling him the gift was a safe one to give to a little girl. He couldn't help thinking the girl's whole future and how she approached it might very well be formed here, in this room, because Santa Claus had had time to fly his reindeer over to her part of the city and bring her a gift.

It was, Keith discovered, a very heady feeling.

And Kenzie had given it to him.

## Chapter Sixteen

"Keep going, Santa," Kenzie urged him, whispering into his ear. The little girl squealed when she discovered a soft, furry yellow bear wearing a red T-shirt beneath the silver-and-green Christmas wrapping paper that she had sent flying in ripped pieces. "It looks like you're on a roll."

"I don't look anything like Santa Claus," he protested. Even with him sitting down, the jacket was pooling around him like a red lake.

"Granted, you're not exactly rotund, but you've got the suit. More importantly, you came in carrying a bag stuffed with toys, so you'll more than do," Kenzie told him. She could see that he needed just a little more convincing. "Try to think of yourself as the poor man's Santa Claus. Or, in this case, the poor child's Santa Claus."

Keith spared her another look as he surrendered. He couldn't very well find it in his heart to argue with that. Not when he was looking down at so many eager little faces.

Besides, he had to admit that seeing the girl smile and hearing her squeal of joy did feel good.

"Okay," he said in the deepest voice he could summon, waving the next child to come closer. "Let's see what's in this bag for you."

He didn't have to say it twice.

"I think you've found his element, Kenzie," her mother said to her as they both observed Keith in this new role. He would hand out a gift only after spending a couple of minutes talking to each new child. Andrea glanced at her before continuing. "He was always polite and well mannered, but this is definitely the happiest I've seen him."

Normally optimistic, exuberant and the first to lead the parade, this one time Kenzie was treading lightly, leery of assuming too much. "Someone once told me something about counting chickens," Kenzie replied, looking pointedly at her mother.

"Perhaps," Andrea conceded. She smiled at her daughter. "But after all, my love, it is Christmas, the season of miracles, and the kids seem more than willing to believe that your friend is Santa Claus."

"Santa Claus after a major crash diet," Kenzie pointed out, nodding at the way Keith's costume hung on his body.

Andrea laughed softly, shaking her head. "What happened to my dreamer?"

"It's uncharted territory, Mom. She decided to tread cautiously," Kenzie answered.

There was deep affection in Andrea's eyes as she looked at her youngest daughter. "So it's like that, is it?"

Kenzie could feel herself retreating, as if saying anything at all would jeopardize this happiness. Until now, she'd never been superstitious, but until now, she'd never felt like this before.

"No, I just—"

Something suddenly popped into Andrea's head. "Wait, isn't he the boy you had that huge crush on?" The moment she said it, it began making a great deal more sense.

Alarmed, Kenzie instantly pulled her mother aside. She was afraid that the next thing out of her mother's mouth would embarrass her beyond any hope of recovery.

"That was then," Kenzie insisted in a very firm, hoarse whisper.

In response, her mother smiled. "I see."

Oh, God, she should have flatly denied it instead. She hated lying, but there were consequences to this getting out. Her mother meant well, but Kenzie had a sinking feeling it would be only a matter of time—short time— before her mother spoke to Keith about "great loves that were meant to be" or something equally as embarrassing.

"Mother—" There was a desperate warning note in Kenzie's voice.

Andrea held her hands up as if that helped establish her innocence. "I didn't say a word, dear," she said. "Well, I have to be getting back. I just came with the toys the way you asked me to. But there's lots to do at home. Don't forget to come tomorrow," she reminded Kenzie as she began to leave. "Bring your friend."

The last sentence floated back to Kenzie in her mother's wake.

"How did you happen to find this place?"

Keith asked her the question when they were back in the shelter's overcrowded main office. The first thing he'd stripped off was the beard, which had been driving him crazy for the past three hours. He ran his hands over his face, trying not to give in to the overwhelming desire to scratch it and keep scratching.

The jacket and oversize pants were next. The last gift

had been given out, and after spending another hour in the children's midst, the children and Santa had parted company. He was tired, but there was an odd sort of contentment weaving its way through him that he had to admit he was enjoying.

Still, he was more than ready to go home.

*Home.*

It felt rather odd, after all this time had passed, to suddenly be applying that word to the house on Normandie Circle. He hadn't thought of it in that sense since he'd left. And yet, somewhere in the back of his mind, he supposed it had always been that. Possibly years from now it would still unofficially wear that label for him even if he never uttered the word again. The house on Normandie had been and would always be home.

Some of that, he knew, had to do with Kenzie. Maybe even a lot of it.

"I didn't exactly find this place," Kenzie was saying, answering his question. "Mrs. Manetti told me about it. She and her crew prepare food and bring it here every other week. Otherwise the shelter serves foods that are donated by discount stores. In her opinion, just because people have temporarily fallen on hard times doesn't mean they should only have three-day-old bread, powdered foods and fruits that were going to be thrown out."

"Mrs. Manetti," he repeated, the name nudging at a memory he couldn't quite get hold of. "Isn't that the woman who—"

"Catered your mother's funeral reception," Kenzie finished his sentence for him. "Yes, she is. She has a very big heart. When I once mentioned that observation to her, she just shrugged it off, saying it's her way of giving back to the community for her own good fortune."

Well, that explained the food he saw being served, but

not everything. "And the toys I was giving out today? Where did they come from?"

Kenzie's smile grew wider. "My mother and sisters have toy drives in their communities."

"Just your mother and sisters?" he questioned, sensing that there was some information missing. There were a lot of toys in that bag. "You don't have any part in it?"

Kenzie never felt comfortable talking about herself when it came to charitable deeds, but he'd asked her a direct question, so she was forced to give him an answer. "I might."

Folding the suit and placing it into the bag that Kenzie had brought it in, he laughed, shaking his head. They walked out of the shelter and got into her car. "I feel like I've just wandered into some old-fashioned feel-good movie."

"No, that'll come tomorrow," she told him glibly, driving away from the shelter.

Caught off guard, Keith looked at her, confused. "Tomorrow? What's tomorrow?"

She did her best to keep a straight face as she asked, "You mean besides being Christmas Eve?"

Keith suppressed a sigh. "Yes, besides being Christmas Eve."

"My mother invited you to the family Christmas party." When he made no response, she added, "I'll be there, too, seeing as how I'm part of the family and all."

"And I'll be on a plane for San Francisco," he told her.

She'd given herself a pep talk centered around the fact that what had happened last night would not change anything—but she hadn't expected it not to change anything so soon. She realized that he was leaving, but she wasn't ready to see him go so quickly.

"Really?" She packed a great deal of feeling into the

single word. "You don't want to be flying on Christmas Eve."

"Why not?" he challenged her. Then he reminded her, "A room full of kids thinks I'm Santa Claus. Santa Claus flies every Christmas Eve."

"Santa Claus doesn't fly," she contradicted him. "The reindeer do. If the reindeer were sitting on a plane, letting some pilot fly them—and you—it might not be all that safe on Christmas Eve. Even the reindeer know the pilot might have been celebrating just a little too much."

They were here, back at the house, she realized. The distance had managed just to disappear. She supposed the thought of his leaving so abruptly had caused her not to notice.

Kenzie pulled up in front of his house.

"You're reaching," he told her as they got out of her car.

The open house sign Mrs. Sommers had placed beside the for sale sign was gone. That meant the house was his again, at least for the night. He tried not to notice the sense of relief that came with the realization. He refused to explore what it might actually mean to him.

"I know, but you're tall. I have to reach," she quipped.

He laughed and shook his head again. "Kenzie, you're one of a kind."

"Considering the business I'm in, I'll take that as a compliment," she told him.

Keith began to go up the front walk. Kenzie, he discovered, was right behind him.

"You're coming in?" he asked, not entirely surprised at how good that thought made him feel.

"Well, I have to see what we'll be putting out for the sale tomorrow." She'd already told him that her aim tomorrow would be to appeal to shoppers who had put off finding the right gift until the last minute. "Besides," she continued as she followed him inside, "it would be kind of difficult for me to make dinner if I'm not in the house."

This was the first he was hearing about it. "You're making dinner?"

Kenzie nodded. "Unless you're rather have takeout, of course."

He had takeout all the time when he worked. He didn't believe in brown-bagging it, and evenings usually found him still at his desk, so ordering takeout seemed like the only logical way to go. But he didn't look forward to it anymore.

"No, I'm fine with you making dinner," he assured her quickly, not wanting her to change her mind. "I don't get much of a chance to eat a home-cooked meal."

Kenzie flashed a smile. She'd been pretty sure she wasn't going to need to twist his arm.

"Home cooked meal it is," she declared.

*And then, maybe dessert*, she added silently, knowing better than to count on it. This was all very undefined territory she was treading.

And maybe she was giving herself too much credit, but she had a strong hunch that he felt the exact same way about what was going on here. The man exuded sex appeal, but she suspected he was completely oblivious to that.

Ninety minutes later, after having seconds and then thirds, Keith realized he was dangerously close to needing to unbuckle his belt, or at least move it by a notch. He was stuffed—but happily so. The meal she had prepared for them—Sicilian chicken—had been so good, he couldn't stop himself from taking "just a little bit more" until "more" had added up to almost three full servings.

"Where did you learn to cook like that?" he asked

her, sitting back in his chair. He didn't want to leave the table just yet.

"Watching my mom," Kenzie replied. "And Mrs. Manetti's given me tips now and then. This was her recipe," she told him.

"How do you know her?" She had managed to arouse his curiosity on so many levels, and since he was asking questions, he figured he might as well throw that one into the mix.

"She and my mom are friends. They have been for a very long time."

As she talked, she began to gather the plates together, consolidating what had been left on the serving platters onto one.

"I think they were each other's bridesmaids. I know my mom was there for her when Mrs. Manetti lost her husband. And Mrs. Manetti returned the favor when my dad died." And then she smiled, remembering. "Mrs. Manetti was the one who encouraged my mother to start her own business, said that was the best way for her to get out into the world again and get on with the business of living. Mrs. Manetti told my mother that starting her own catering company was what really helped her function again."

"They both sound like extraordinary women," he told her. Accompanying the words was a pang he was quick to bury.

He had a strong feeling that if he didn't get up and start moving, he was going to wind up falling asleep right where he sat. Keith rose from the table and picked up his plate, taking it to the sink.

Kenzie was on her feet as well, carrying the platter to the counter. She covered it and placed it in the refrigerator.

"Most moms usually are," she told him, commenting on his observation.

She went back for the other plates, putting those in the sink on top of his plate.

Keith turned away from her. "Yes, well, we might have a difference of opinion on that," he said. There was a faint touch of bitterness in his voice.

What could have gone down between his mother and Keith to have made him so angry, even now, after her death? she wondered. Her sympathy went out to both.

"Some just don't have as easy a time of it as others," she told him.

Kenzie was really afraid this was going to eat straight into his gut. Putting her hands on his shoulders, she turned Keith around to face her. "It's Christmas, Keith. Don't you think it's time you forgave her?"

He was *not* about to get into this with her. He didn't want to spoil the evening—or the upbeat feeling that today and playing Santa Claus for the children had created.

"I don't want to talk about that now," he told her firmly.

Kenzie prided herself on knowing when to back off. "Fair enough. What do you want to talk about?"

That was the moment when he gave in to impulse, which he wasn't accustomed to doing. But then, none of what had been happening these last few days could be categorized as normal for him.

"We'll think of something," he told Kenzie just before he pulled her close and kissed her the way he had been aching to do all day long.

It didn't end there, as they both knew it wouldn't. Instead, one kiss blossomed into two, then three, then four, each kiss lasting longer, going deeper than the one before it.

Passions and desires instantly reheated in their blood, laying open the path that they had accidentally discovered last night. Except this time, there was no resistance, no hesitancy. Instead, there was the immediate joy of encountering the new and yet familiar feelings and reactions to the wondrous brand-new world that was waiting for them just a whisper of a shadow away.

A world neither one of them even tried to resist this time.

Resistance was futile, Kenzie caught herself thinking, remembering a clichéd line from a classic sci-fi series. Keith was making her close to crazy as he caused desire and gratification to leap almost simultaneously through her body.

She returned the favor as best she could, all too aware of the ironic fact that each moment she spent with him was one less moment she had left to spend with him. Unless something drastic happened to change his mind, he would be leaving her very soon.

He'd changed his mind about leaving tomorrow. He was going with her to the party at her mother's.

But what of the day after tomorrow? a small voice in her head—or was that her heart?—whispered.

And as they came together, creating that wondrous, temporary paradise for each other that she craved, she was left to wonder if she could stand watching him actually leave her.

She knew the answer to that even if she didn't want to admit it to herself.

Spent, exhausted, she lay beside Keith, missing him already.

"Wow," he murmured a moment later, too tired to pretend to be unaffected. "A few more times like that and I very well might not be able to move again." He felt her mouth curving in a smile against his chest as he held her. "What?" he asked, curious what had made her smile like that.

Curious, he realized, about everything having to do with her. Dangerous thoughts for a man who was leaving the day after tomorrow, he silently warned. Not just leaving, but for all intents and purpose, never returning to the region again.

"You just gave me an idea," she told him, her eyes dancing as she raised herself up on her elbow, her hair brushing tantalizingly along his skin.

He wasn't even sure just what he'd said, much less what it might have suggested to her. "What kind of an idea?" he asked.

"I plan to love you into a stupor." *So you can't leave.* "I don't want to waste my breath talking." She curled her body along his like a seductive snake.

"What do you want to waste it on?" he heard himself asking.

She was smiling into his eyes just before she answered him—kind of.

"Guess."

And then she didn't give him a chance to say anything further. He couldn't if he'd wanted to. Her mouth was sealed to his, creating blissful havoc.

## Chapter Seventeen

It felt strange waking up beside her. Strange how very right it felt, even though he'd never allowed his barriers to be lowered to this extent, never spent the night with any woman he had made love with. Spending the night whispered of the beginnings of a commitment. And a commitment was something he had never wanted, never allowed himself to want.

And yet, here he was, of his own free will, finding a certain sort of comfort in the simple act of listening to her breathe.

*Well, don't get used to it. You're leaving tomorrow, remember? If you don't, if you keep finding excuses to hang around, you're going to regret it. You know that you will.*

His arm tightened around Kenzie, as if that could somehow hold reality—his reality—at bay a little while longer.

At least just for today.

He felt Kenzie stirring beside him. The next moment, her eyes opened and she smiled at him. "Hi."

Everything inside him smiled back at her.

"Hi yourself." He did his best not to sound distracted or give her any indication of the war that was currently being waged within him. "I didn't wake you, did I?" he asked, his arm automatically tightening around her when he thought about leaving Kenzie.

"I don't know," Kenzie admitted sleepily. "Did you shake me?"

"No." Technically, he hadn't, he told himself, knowing he was falling back on semantics.

"Then I guess you didn't wake me." Kenzie stretched, stifling a yawn, unaware of how sensual she looked or how something as simple as her stretching like that was arousing him. "Want breakfast?"

"Eventually," he told her, drawing her back into his arms.

And just like that, Kenzie was wide awake. "Oh. Dessert first," she said with approval, her eyes shining. "Good. I like dessert."

"You talk too much, Kenzie," he told her, beginning to kiss the sides of her neck and causing those delicious sensations to start leaping through her.

"So I've been told," Kenzie murmured just before he brought his mouth to hers and she couldn't say another word—and didn't want to.


"I was beginning to think you two weren't coming," Andrea said, opening the door to admit her daughter and Keith.

She hugged each warmly, starting with Keith, before either of them even had a chance to cross the threshold into the house.

Kenzie exchanged glances with Keith, her mouth curving as she thought of what had delayed them. "Wrapping presents took longer than we anticipated," she explained.

"*Wrapping* presents," Andrea repeated.

The expression on her mother's face told Kenzie that she wasn't fooled for a minute—and she couldn't have been more pleased about it.

*Don't get used to it, Mom. He's leaving on a jet plane come tomorrow—or the day after, but he is leaving, just like the song says*, she thought sadly.

Kenzie wasn't altogether sure if the silent caution echoing in her head was meant for her mother or for her.

Even standing here amid the warmth of family, with Keith right next to her, she could feel the ache beginning.

God, but she didn't want him to go.

"Well," Andrea was saying, hooking one arm through each of theirs, "as long as you're both finally here, that's all that counts." She beamed at each in turn, then announced, "It's official. We can start the Christmas party now."

"Your mother's kidding, right?" Keith said to her the moment Andrea moved on. "She really didn't mean she was holding up the party until we got here—did she?" he asked skeptically.

She would have loved to have reassured him—or, even simpler, pretended not to know the answer to his question. But if their time together was limited, she wouldn't mar it by lying, even though the answer would probably make him uneasy.

"My mother is a very happy, upbeat person, but certain things she doesn't kid about. Christmas parties aren't complete until everyone in the family attends. She's been like that ever since I can remember."

That might have been true, but in his opinion, Kenzie

seemed to be overlooking one very salient point. "I'm not family."

She shrugged as if the matter was out of her hands. "Apparently, you are—for tonight."

Maybe he shouldn't have come, after all, Keith thought. He was only getting further entrenched in a situation he had no business being in. He shouldn't allow her family to see him in a light that wasn't anywhere near accurate— no matter how seductive that light might temporarily be to him.

The next moment, however, as he was swept up in the festivities, the thought, born of self-preservation, vanished.

"Your mother shouldn't have bought me presents," he protested late that night when he and Kenzie had returned to his house.

"Don't worry about it," Kenzie assured him. "My mother loves buying presents. It makes her happy." She slipped off her coat and let it drape over the back of the sofa. She laced her hands through his as she looked up into his face, desperately trying not to think beyond the moment. "Consider it helping her find a reason to satisfy her shopping craving."

He shook his head as he marveled, "You know, the way you can twist things around until they fit the occasion, you would make quite a lawyer."

Kenzie demurred having the label applied to her. "Uh-uh, not my style. People don't like lawyers." She managed to get the line out while keeping a straight face.

He ran the back of his hand along her cheek. "Until they need one."

Kenzie could already feel herself melting. "Good point. And I suddenly find myself in desperate need of one."

Dropping his hands, she draped her arms around the back of his neck. She leaned into him just enough to have all the vital parts of their bodies touch. She could feel the sparks being set off already.

"And why would you be in desperate need of a lawyer?" he teased.

"Because we're standing under mistletoe." Kenzie grinned as she pointed over his head. "And I have this overwhelming, uncontrollable urge to kiss a lawyer."

Curious, he looked up. Kenzie was right. There *was* mistletoe hanging from the light fixture, and it was directly over their heads. He was certain the mistletoe hadn't been there when'd they left for her mother's party.

Or had it?

"Who put that there?" he asked her.

Her shoulders rose and fell in complete innocence. "Elves?" she guessed. "Enough with the small talk," Kenzie told him. "Like I said, I have this sudden need to fulfill a fantasy and kiss a lawyer."

Tomorrow he just might be on that flight back to the rest of his life. But he was still here tonight, and it was up to him to make the very most of every second he had. So he shoved the oppressive weight of his thoughts aside and did his best to grab a festive attitude.

"At your service, ma'am," he told her, closing his arms around Kenzie.

Her eyes shone as she replied, "I certainly hope so." And then she put him to the test.

It wasn't supposed to be this hard, Keith told himself early the next morning—Christmas morning. He should have been gone several days ago, not lingering like this, looking for yet another excuse to stay a day longer.

He had a life waiting for him in San Francisco, he silently insisted. A career to get back to. Here he was just floating around in limbo.

The bulk of his mother's possessions had already been sold and picked up, thanks to Kenzie's unique ability to sell ice to polar bears. What was left he'd decided to donate to the shelter where Kenzie volunteered rather than have her try to sell it on consignment at her shop.

He hadn't been sure how she would react to that when he proposed it on the way home last night. The straight donation meant she wouldn't be getting a percentage of the sale. But Kenzie, being Kenzie, had been happy about his decision.

"It's the right thing to do," she'd told him. "Trust me, it'll mean a lot more to someone at the shelter than it would to some shopper who'll most likely leave what she bought in her garage or the back of her closet once the novelty wears off."

The house, on the other hand, didn't seem to be generating enough interest, which in turn meant it wasn't about to sell soon. But then, given the season and what Mrs. Sommers had told him, Keith had to admit he wasn't really surprised. Since he didn't need the money, there was no urgency to sell the house.

There was also no need for him to hang around.

No real need except that he wanted to.

Which was why he needed to leave. Needed to leave *now*, before Kenzie looked at him and said something that would make him weaken. That would make him stay.

So while Kenzie ran an errand—dropping off Christmas gifts at the homes of the two assistants who worked for her—Keith packed his suitcase.

He'd almost given in to the temptation to leave before she returned—it would mean having to spend an extra hour at the airport, but then at least the break would be a clean one.

At the last moment, he decided to tell her goodbye in person. She deserved that.

Anything else would have been cowardly. Maybe it was vanity on his part, but he didn't want Kenzie to remember him that way—being too cowardly to face her. So he stayed, giving her an hour, waiting for the sound of her turning the doorknob and returning.

Waiting was agony.

And then he heard her opening the door.

The moment she walked in, Kenzie understood.

She didn't even have to see the suitcase standing on the floor behind the coffee table to know that Keith was leaving. And it wasn't even the suit he had on that gave him away. The expression on his face did it, the somber look in his eyes.

Her heart drained, her head throbbing, she started talking without comprehending what would come out of her mouth.

"You're leaving early," she said.

"No," he contradicted her, the word feeling wooden in his mouth, "I'm leaving late. I should have left two days ago. But I bumped back the ticket."

She knew that already. She'd overheard him doing it and kept praying he'd do it again—or throw away the ticket altogether.

This was where she had an opportunity to save face, to say something blasé and glib. This was where she began to distance herself from him.

She couldn't do it. Couldn't be anything but honest with him. The other facade wouldn't have been her. "I was hoping you bumped it back until the day after New Year's."

Not that he hadn't been tempted, but it would have been even harder with that much more time going by. "I would still have to leave," he pointed out.

"Maybe," she conceded. "But it wouldn't be today," she told him quietly.

Logic. He had to hang onto logic. Emotions would be his downfall. "Kenzie, I don't live here anymore."

She pressed her lips together, obviously trying not to cry. "I know." The words came out in a whisper.

If he'd left already, he wouldn't have to be agonizing through this conversation now. He didn't want to see her hurting. "My law firm is in San Francisco."

"I know," Kenzie repeated almost stoically.

His cell phone rang just then, and he glanced down at his pocket as if the phone was intruding.

"Better get that," she told him stiffly. "Might be your firm wanting to know what's keeping you."

*You. What's keeping me is you*, Keith told her silently.

But he knew that was exactly why he had to leave today. Leave *now*. Because if he didn't, he might not go at all, and he had to. Otherwise he wouldn't be who he really was.

So he turned away to answer his cell, trying to regroup. He didn't want to make this any harder for either of them.

Moving aside, he took his phone out of his pocket and glanced at the caller ID. Kenzie was right. One of the firm's senior partners was having his secretary call him, no doubt to verify that he would be on the five o'clock flight out of John Wayne Airport.

"Hello," he snapped. "This is O'Connell." And then he listened to the woman on the other end for a minute. Her end of the conversation was very sparse. And predictable.

"I'll be on it," he told the woman, his throat feeling incredibly dry as he forced the words out. He ended the call and tucked the phone back into his pocket before turning around to face Kenzie again.

He was stalling because he didn't know what to say to her or how to say it. The idea of the getaway he'd turned his back on earlier began to feel like a missed opportunity.

That didn't change the fact that he still had to get through this. Taking a breath, he forced himself to speak.

"I guess this is it," he began.

"I guess so," she agreed stiffly, her dry tone matching his.

He had to be honest with her even though he wanted to say anything that would take that stricken but brave look off her face. "I won't tell you I'll be back, because I don't know if I will. Maybe I'll have to come back when Mrs. Sommers sells the house—"

"She can mail you the papers," Kenzie said, her tone implying that there was no reason for him to return—at least, not if that was his only reason for coming back.

"I guess she can," he agreed.

With nothing left to stop him, Keith picked up his suitcase. More than anything, he wanted to take her into his arms, to kiss her one last time—long and hard, because this kiss was going to have to last him. But if he stopped to kiss her like that, he was fairly certain that he wouldn't make it out the door.

So instead, his hand just tightened around his suitcase—he did it to keep from grabbing her. "Goodbye, Kenzie. Thanks for everything."

She could feel the tears beginning to gather in her eyes. Damn it, Keith needed to leave before she broke down altogether. She didn't want him to see her crying. Didn't want him to think it was some cheap feminine ploy. Most of all, she didn't want to break down because if he saw her crying and still walked away, she knew she couldn't survive that sort of heartbreak.

So rather than make a comment, or give in to her natural instincts and throw her arms around him, or kiss him goodbye while saying something to him that she would regret, Kenzie just said goodbye and walked out the door ahead of him, her head held high.

She didn't pause to glance back, to see if he was watching her. She just looked straight ahead and walked as quickly as she could to her car. The second she got in, she closed the door.

Turning the key, she started the vehicle, telling herself over and over again not to cry until she had at least gotten out of his cul-de-sac.

She didn't quite make it.

The tears started coming before she had a chance to make the left turn onto the through street that ultimately led out of the development. Blinking madly didn't keep them at bay, didn't curb the flow.

A part of her had clung to the hope that he'd change his mind at the last minute.

But he hadn't.

Keith stood in his driveway, watching her drive away, struggling with the very strong desire to run after her and make her turn the car around and come back.

To what end? he asked himself. He had to leave. An extra hour or even an extra day wasn't going to change that. Being here in Bedford wasn't what his life was about anymore. He'd forged a new life for himself in San Francisco. It had taken him ten years to do it, but it was solid now and he had a commitment to the firm he worked for.

He couldn't just contemplate throwing all that away on a whim because he'd had an unexpectedly nice eight days here. People went away to exotic places on vacation, but they didn't suddenly uproot their entire lives and move there just because they had had a nice few days. That would have been completely crazy.

He knew better than that.

He knew exactly what he was leaving and what was waiting for him when the plane landed.

He knew.

Keith's hands tightened on the steering wheel as he pressed down harder on the accelerator. He told himself not to think because right now that would only serve to confuse matters.

Most of all, he told himself not to feel.

That used to be a lot easier to do when he had nothing to feel about, he thought.

Keith stepped on the gas harder, going faster. Trying to outrun his thoughts before they could catch up to him and make him turn around again.

## Chapter Eighteen

Maizie hadn't intended to stop at the house on Normandie. She was just driving by to see if the flyers in the clear container beneath the for sale sign on the front lawn needed to be replenished. But when she saw Kenzie's car parked in the driveway, she pulled her own up to the curb just past the mailbox and got out.

The front door was locked, so she used her passkey, knocking as she slowly opened the door. She didn't want to walk in on something she shouldn't.

"Kenzie, are you in here?" she called out.

In response, a rather tired-looking Kenzie came out into the living room from the kitchen. "Right here, Mrs. Sommers."

There was a sadness about Kenzie that she immediately noticed. It went far beyond the smile the young woman was attempting to maintain. Maizie's first impulse was to ask her what was wrong, but she refrained. Kenzie would tell her if she wanted her to know.

Walking into the house, Maizie said, "I haven't seen Keith around for a few days now. Would you know where he is?"

She'd held two more open house events for this property. At the moment, all her other properties had gone into escrow or the owners had decided to hold off any further dealings until after the holidays, so she was concentrating the preponderance of her sale efforts on this house.

There'd been some foot traffic, but that had consisted mainly of people who were just curious, or were looking for new decorating ideas, or made a habit out of frequenting open houses, poking around the rooms to see how other people lived.

She hadn't seen Keith either of those days, but today, apparently Kenzie had come by to set up the last of the estate sales before having the rest of the furniture removed and given to charity. Quite honestly, Maizie had stopped when she saw her car because she was curious about how the two were getting along.

"He's home," Kenzie replied, doing her best to sound upbeat and friendly. She had a sinking feeling she was failing.

Maizie glanced over the younger woman's shoulder toward the rest of the house. Since Keith obviously wasn't here, she made the only logical assumption. "He's at your home?"

"No, his home," Kenzie replied stoically. "In San Francisco."

"Oh." Maizie searched her face, finding the answer before she asked. "When is he coming back?"

"I have no idea," Kenzie replied. She was doing her best not to let her voice crack, but it was getting harder and harder not to break down. "I don't think he's coming back."

"Oh, my dear, I am so sorry." Ever maternal, Maizie slipped her arm around the younger woman's shoulders. "How do you feel?" she asked, concerned since, after all, she had been the driving force behind bringing the two together.

Could she have been this wrong about them?

Kenzie wanted to say "Fine." She really did. In lieu of that, she would have said, "Okay." But the word that wound up coming out of her mouth was *"Lousy."*

"Oh, honey." Maizie's voice was filled with sympathy as she gave her another heartfelt squeeze. She did a quick review in her mind of all the instances she'd seen the two together. "Maybe he just needs a little time to wrap things up. I saw the way that man looked at you. A man doesn't look at a woman that way if he isn't really involved with her."

But Kenzie shook her head. No more delusions. She was determined to see clearly now, to see their relationship the way it was.

"I appreciate what you're trying to do, Mrs. Sommers. But I think you're wrong."

Stepping away from the older woman's comforting embrace, Kenzie snatched up her purse. The heck with the rest of the sale. She had to leave before she started crying. She absolutely refused to break down in front of anyone, even if that person was the most sympathetic person she had ever met besides her own mother.

She didn't want sympathy, Kenzie thought as she left the house. She wanted not to care. Most of all, she wanted not to ache so much.

Keith went into his firm's main office the morning after he arrived back. He went in early, stayed late and for the most part picked up his life just where he had left off.

Except that it didn't quite feel like his life. It felt more like a shell—a hollow, ill-fitting shell without depth, without dimensions.

Without substance.

He told himself that was because he'd had an unnatural break in his routine. Having his dormant emotions shaken up the way he had was a lot to deal with, and it would take a little time for things to get back to normal.

His normal.

Time. That was all he needed. Time.

Keith kept doggedly at it for two more days, trying to recapture the rhythm he felt he'd lost by going back to Bedford.

After the third day of almost nonstop work, he finally remembered to unpack. The suitcase had been standing by the front door all this time as if to remind him that he could just as easily take it to his car as up the stairs.

His car, he sternly told himself, was not an option. The only reason the suitcase would find its way to the car was if he were going to the airport—which he wasn't.

He took the suitcase upstairs.

Once there, he brought it to his bedroom and laid it on his bed. Snapping the locks open, he forced himself to concentrate on the mechanics of unpacking rather than allowing his mind to stray to a place more than four hundred miles away.

Being with Kenzie had been great, but it was over, he silently reminded himself. His time with her had just been a commercial in the program of his life, and he had to remember that.

Remember that he had worked—

Keith stopped dead, staring into his suitcase. Specifically, staring at what was right on top of his shirts.

Where had those come from?

He hadn't packed them, hadn't even *touched* them.

Letters covered the entire width and breadth of his suitcase. The moment he opened it, they began cascading out. They were the letters Kenzie had found, written by his mother. He picked one up.

The same letters he had told Kenzie to throw out.

"Kenzie, what are you trying to do to me? I said I didn't want to read them!" he shouted at the woman who was four hundred miles away.

Scooping up the letters into his arms, Keith threw them into the wastepaper basket in his bathroom.

As if in rebellion, the letters overwhelmed the container, and the basket just fell over on its side. The letters covered the basket rather than winding up inside it.

He cursed at the pile—and the woman who had snuck the letters into his suitcase—and stormed away.

When had she put those letters in there? Keith silently demanded, mystified. It had to have been just before he left the house. He'd had the suitcase open just prior to that, while he was packing, and his cell phone had rung. He'd turned away to talk. It must have happened then. If she'd snuck them into his suitcase sometime before, he would have seen the letters while he was packing.

The next question that occurred to him in giant neon letters was, *why* would she do this to him? Why would she actually pack up his old memories so that he'd be forced to confront them when he opened the suitcase?

Had she done it because he had chosen to leave her? Was forcing the letters to his attention her way of punishing him for going?

Despite what he would have labeled as evidence if this were a court of law, Keith couldn't bring himself to believe Kenzie would have done it for such a hurtful reason.

The Kenzie he knew didn't punish people, didn't seek revenge, no matter what.

*The Kenzie you knew? How well does anyone know anyone? You were together a total of seven days. Not exactly a lifetime, is it—unless you're a fruit fly*, he mocked himself.

Keith sat on the edge of his bed, staring angrily into his bathroom at the letters that were lying all over the wastebasket and the floor.

It was a dirty trick. Leaving Bedford—and Kenzie—was obviously the right thing to do.

This proved it.

She wasn't going to answer the knock on the door. She'd already begged off from attending the New Year's Eve party her brother was having, giving what she deemed was an Academy Award–worthy performance. She called in her regrets, sniffling and coughing as she pretended to be coming down with the flu.

She repeated her performance two more times—once for her pregnant sister, whom she had assured didn't want to be near someone coming down with the flu, and once for her mother, who had been alerted about her planned no-show by the others.

Her mother had been a harder sell. Andrea offered to forgo the party and ring in the new year with her and a hot bowl of homemade chicken soup. Since her mother made the world's best chicken soup, it had been a hard offer for her to refuse, given how she truly felt. The chicken soup would have been comforting.

But ultimately Kenzie managed to convince her mother that she was just too wiped out for any company. Besides, if her mother skipped the party "to hold my hot, sweaty hand, I'll never forgive myself." After a considerable amount of rhetoric had gone back and forth, Andrea relented and promised to have a good time for both of them.

"But I'll be by in the morning to check in on you," her mother added.

"Come at your own risk," Kenzie had told her, then sneezed. "I'll be here."

"Risk. Right." Andrea laughed. "Like I didn't nurse all five of you kids through coughs, colds, the flu and heaven only knows what all else. Get into bed, Kenzie, and get your rest. I'll see you tomorrow."

"Yes, Mom," Kenzie dutifully replied.

She hated lying like this, but she just couldn't take a room full of noisy family right now, all trying to cheer her up. Her sisters would probably offer to make a voodoo doll resembling Keith. She wasn't up to that, either.

She didn't want revenge. She just wanted him.

"And Happy New Year," her mother said before hanging up.

"Happy New Year," Kenzie echoed, disheartened. The last thing the new year would be was happy, Kenzie had thought as she put her cell phone away.

An hour later, she'd felt no different. But her mother obviously did, because that had to be her at the door, determined to feed her and try to raise her mood.

Kenzie was down to her last nerve, and she was in no mood to go on with her pretense.

So she decided to wait her mother out, ignoring the knocking that had only grown louder, in hopes that the woman would assume she was asleep, give up and go home. She had left only one fifteen-watt bulb on, so it certainly looked as if she'd gone to bed.

The fourth round of knocking told her that her mother wasn't giving up.

With a sigh, Kenzie got into character and shuffled to the door.

"There was no reason for you to come," Kenzie said in between coughs as she unlocked the door and opened it just a crack. She was still hoping to convince her mother to turn around and go home.

"We've got a slight difference of opinion on that," Keith told her just before he opened the door farther and walked in.

Stunned, Kenzie had let go of the door and stepped back, staring at Keith and wondering if she'd fallen asleep on the sofa and this was just a dream she was having.

"That was a lousy thing to do," Keith told her as he turned to face her.

Her mind scrambled.

The letters. He was talking about the letters.

"I'm sorry," she said, "but I thought you'd wind up regretting not reading them."

"Them?" he repeated as he looked at Kenzie, confused.

"The letters. That's what you're talking about, isn't it?"

He laughed shortly, his irritation coming through. "No."

"Then I don't understand," she admitted. She was too tired to try to talk her way out of anything. Two hours of crying had taken a huge toll on her brain capacity. "What's this lousy thing I did?"

"Like you don't know," he accused her. "You let me leave. You let me go four hundred miles away from you to find out that I didn't *want* to be four hundred miles away from you."

Kenzie stared at him, trying to make sense out of what he was saying and get it to jibe with the look she saw on his face.

"Are you happy or angry that you're here?" she asked.

"Can't you tell? I'm happy," he all but shouted at her.

At that moment, the solid wall of tension growing inside her began to disintegrate. "Could have fooled me," she told him.

"Why not?" he countered. "I tried to fool me. I tried to fool myself into believing I didn't want to be here. That being with you for seven days was enough and I didn't need any more. Well, I do," he told her firmly. "I need more. Lots more."

That persistent kernel of hope she had never been entirely successful at dissolving just popped inside her chest, spreading out to fill every single nook and cranny within her.

This time her smile was genuine. "How much more?" she asked.

"Does the word *forever* mean anything to you?" Keith asked.

Her smile went from ear to ear. Further, if possible. "Yeah. Heaven."

"Funny, me, too," Keith responded, drawing her into his arms.

God, it felt wonderful being held in his arms like this. It was where she knew she belonged. "What did you do with the letters?"

Keith looked into her eyes. He loved her. How could he have missed that? Or ever thought he could walk away from it when people spent their whole lives looking for what had just dropped into his lap? Was he crazy?

No, definitely not crazy—because this time, he was staying.

"What most people do with letters," he told her. "I read them. And I wish she'd sent them. If she went through the trouble of writing them, why wouldn't she have sent them?"

"Maybe she was afraid you wouldn't read them," Kenzie told him.

He really couldn't argue with that. Because even now, he'd almost thrown them out. "Yeah, maybe," he agreed. "I love you, Kenzie."

Her heart swelled almost to bursting. "I love you back." And then, because she was desperately trying not to dissolve in happy tears, she pretended to be playful as she asked, "So, now what?"

"You mean after I make love with you?"

Her smile could have lit up a corner of the entire city. "Yes."

He shrugged nonchalantly. "I do it again."

"And then?"

He grew serious. "I don't know. But we'll figure it out. As long as I have you, the details don't really matter."

What he was saying suddenly hit her. She looked at him, stunned. "You're leaving your firm?"

He nodded. "I already did."

She couldn't let him do that for her. He wouldn't be happy doing nothing. He was a man who needed goals to work toward. "Keith, you can't do that. You won't last a day not working."

"Who says I won't be working?" he asked. Before she could say anything, he continued. "One of the things my mother and I fought about before I left home was that I wanted to go into corporate law and my mother wanted me to go into some form of legal aid. She wanted me to help people who couldn't afford to hire a lawyer to represent them. I balked at that, saying that wasn't a way to earn a living. But now, looking back, I think maybe she had the right idea, after all. Besides, I've already earned a lot of money. How much more money does a person need?"

A minute ago, she hadn't thought it was possible to love him more than she did—but she was wrong. "Your mother would have been very proud of you."

He brushed his lips against Kenzie's, then paused for one last moment. This needed to be said. "Thank you for not throwing the letters out the way I told you to."

She'd known from the moment she found them that getting him to read the letters was the right thing to do. But packing them in his suitcase had been her last ditch play—her Hail Mary—to get him to reconsider and come back.

If her attempt had wound up failing, she would have known Keith wasn't the man she thought he was, after all.

But he was.

Kenzie laughed, weaving her arms around his neck. "Anytime you want someone not to do what you tell her to, I'm your woman."

*I'm your woman.*

He liked the sound of that.

"I'm going to hold you to that last part," Keith said just before he stopped all dialogue between them for a very long time.

## *Epilogue*

Maizie Sommers was beaming as she slipped into the fourth pew from the front and took her place beside her two best friends.

She knew she looked like the proverbial cat who swallowed the canary, but she strongly felt she had good reason.

"I told you I was never wrong," she said in a low, very satisfied whisper.

Theresa turned to glance at her. "What are you talking about?"

"And whom are you talking to?" Cecilia asked, leaning forward to peer around Theresa and look at Maizie.

Maizie realized she sounded as if she were talking to herself. Thinking quickly, she rectified that.

"To both of you, of course, and I'm talking about Kenzie. About the last conversation we had just before New Year's Eve. She told me Keith had gone back to San Francisco the day after Christmas and she didn't think he was coming back. I told her I thought he was, and that was when Kenzie told me she thought I was wrong."

"And you said you never were," Theresa guessed. She and Cecilia exchanged glances. That was Maizie all right, confident—and with good reason, really, she thought proudly.

But Cecilia couldn't resist the opportunity to tease her. "What's the view like from Mount Olympus?" she asked.

The strains of the wedding march were just beginning, and the crowd rose to their feet to await the bride's appearance.

"The view is just fantastic," Maizie assured her friends just as the double doors at the rear of the church opened.

As the music swelled, Kenzie appeared on the arm of her oldest brother.

Maizie looked from the bride to the altar, where Keith stood beside Kenzie's other brother. The groom seemed completely mesmerized as he watched his bride coming toward him.

Mesmerized and incredibly happy.

If ever two people looked to be in love, it was these two, Maizie thought, the latest couple she and her friends had successfully matched.

"Absolutely fantastic," Maizie affirmed.

It was hard to tell who looked happiest, Theresa thought, taking in the scene: the bride, the groom—or Maizie.

The logical answer, Theresa decided, was all three.

\* \* \* \* \*

# COMING NEXT MONTH FROM

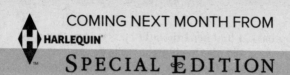

**H** HARLEQUIN®

# SPECIAL EDITION

## Available November 17, 2015

### #2443 A COLD CREEK CHRISTMAS STORY
*Cowboys of Cold Creek* • by RaeAnne Thayne

When librarian Celeste Nichols's children's book becomes a success, she's stunned. Enter Flynn Delaney, her childhood crush, and his young daughter, who could use some of Celeste's storytelling magic since her mother passed away. With the help of Cupid and Santa, this trio might just have the best Christmas yet!

### #2444 CARTER BRAVO'S CHRISTMAS BRIDE
*The Bravos of Justice Creek* • by Christine Rimmer

Carter Bravo wants to settle down...but he's not looking for love. So he asks his best friend, Paige Kettleman, to be his fiancée on a trial basis. What could go wrong? Neither Carter nor Paige can imagine that unexpected love is Santa's gift to them this year!

### #2445 MERRY CHRISTMAS, BABY MAVERICK!
*Montana Mavericks: What Happened at the Wedding?*
by Brenda Harlen

Rust Creek Falls' top secret gossip columnist, Kayla Dalton, has the inside scoop on her high school crush, Trey Strickland. The Thunder Canyon cowboy is going to be a daddy! How does she know? Because she's pregnant with his baby!

### #2446 A PRINCESS UNDER THE MISTLETOE
*Royal Babies* • by Leanne Banks

To protect herself, Princess Sasha Tarisse goes incognito as a nanny to handsome widower Gavin Sinclair's two young children. But what happens when the damsel-in-disguise and the dashing dad fall for one another under the mistletoe?

### #2447 CHRISTMAS ON THE SILVER HORN RANCH
*Men of the West* • by Stella Bagwell

Injured rancher Bowie Calhoun claims he doesn't need a nurse, but he changes his mind when he sees gorgeous Ava Archer. Despite the sparks flying, the beautiful widow tries to keep her distance from the reckless playboy: she wants a family, not a fling! But not even Ava can resist the pull of true love...

### #2448 HIGH COUNTRY CHRISTMAS
*The Brands of Montana* • by Joanna Sims

Cowboy Tyler Brand lives a carefree life—so he's shocked when his fling with London Davenport produces a baby-to-be. The Montana man is determined to do right by London, but she's got secrets aplenty to keep them apart. It'll take a Christmas miracle to get these two together forever!

---

**YOU CAN FIND MORE INFORMATION ON UPCOMING HARLEQUIN® TITLES, FREE EXCERPTS AND MORE AT WWW.HARLEQUIN.COM.**

HSECNM1115

Turn your love of reading into
rewards you'll love with

# Harlequin My Rewards

**Join for FREE today at
www.HarlequinMyRewards.com**

Earn **FREE BOOKS** of your choice.

Experience **EXCLUSIVE OFFERS** and contests.

Enjoy **BOOK RECOMMENDATIONS**
selected just for you.

**PLUS!** Sign up now
and get **500** points
right away!

Earn
**FREE**
REWARDS
Join
Today!
HarlequinMyRewards.com

MYR16R

SPECIAL EXCERPT FROM

**H** HARLEQUIN®

## SPECIAL EDITION

*Quiet librarian Celeste Nichols doesn't expect the success of her children's book. But even more surprising is the family she finds under the mistletoe this year with childhood crush Flynn Delaney and his daughter!*

*Read on for a sneak preview of*
*A COLD CREEK CHRISTMAS STORY, the latest book in RaeAnne Thayne's fan-favorite series,*
**THE COWBOYS OF COLD CREEK***.*

"Okay," Olivia said in a dejected voice. "Thank you for bringing me down here to meet Sparkle and play with the puppies."

"You are very welcome," Celeste said. "Any time you want to come back, we would love to have you. Sparkle would, too."

Olivia seemed heartened by that as she headed for the reindeer's stall one last time.

"Bye, Sparkle. Bye!"

The reindeer nodded his head two or three times as if he were bowing, which made the girl giggle.

Celeste led the way out of the barn. Another inch of snow had fallen during the short time they had been inside, and they walked in silence to where Flynn's SUV was parked in front of the house.

She wrapped her coat around herself while Flynn helped his daughter into the backseat. Once Olivia was settled, he closed the door and turned to Celeste.

"Please tell your family thank-you for inviting me to dinner. I enjoyed it very much."

"I will. Good night."

With a wave, he hopped into his SUV and backed out of the driveway.

She watched them for just a moment, snow settling on her hair and her cheeks while she tried to ignore that little ache in her heart.

She could do this. She was tougher than she sometimes gave herself credit. Yes, she might already care about Olivia and be right on the brink of falling hard for her father. That didn't mean she had to lean forward and leave solid ground.

She would simply have to keep herself centered, focused on her family and her friends, her work and her writing and the holidays. She would do her best to keep him at arm's length. It was the only smart choice if she wanted to emerge unscathed after this holiday season.

Soon they would be gone, and her life would return to the comfortable routine she had created for herself.

As she walked into the house, she tried not to think about how unappealing she suddenly found that idea.

*Don't miss*
*A COLD CREEK CHRISTMAS STORY by*
New York Times *bestselling author RaeAnne Thayne,*
*available December 2015 wherever*
*Harlequin® Special Edition books*
*and ebooks are sold.*

www.Harlequin.com

Copyright ©2015 by RaeAnne Thayne

HSEEXP1115

# REQUEST YOUR FREE BOOKS!

## 2 FREE NOVELS PLUS 2 FREE GIFTS!

### ⒽHARLEQUIN®

# SPECIAL EDITION

## Life, Love & Family

**YES!** Please send me 2 FREE Harlequin® Special Edition novels and my 2 FREE gifts (gifts are worth about $10). After receiving them, if I don't wish to receive any more books, I can return the shipping statement marked "cancel." If I don't cancel, I will receive 6 brand-new novels every month and be billed just $4.74 per book in the U.S. or $5.49 per book in Canada. That's a savings of at least 12% off the cover price! It's quite a bargain! Shipping and handling is just 50¢ per book in the U.S. and 75¢ per book in Canada.* I understand that accepting the 2 free books and gifts places me under no obligation to buy anything. I can always return a shipment and cancel at any time. Even if I never buy another book, the two free books and gifts are mine to keep forever.

235/335 HDN GH3Z

Name _____ (PLEASE PRINT)

Address _____ Apt. #

City _____ State/Prov. _____ Zip/Postal Code

Signature (if under 18, a parent or guardian must sign)

### Mail to the **Reader Service:**
**IN U.S.A.:** P.O. Box 1867, Buffalo, NY 14240-1867
**IN CANADA:** P.O. Box 609, Fort Erie, Ontario L2A 5X3

**Want to try two free books from another line?**
**Call 1-800-873-8635 or visit www.ReaderService.com.**

* Terms and prices subject to change without notice. Prices do not include applicable taxes. Sales tax applicable in N.Y. Canadian residents will be charged applicable taxes. Offer not valid in Quebec. This offer is limited to one order per household. Not valid for current subscribers to Harlequin Special Edition books. All orders subject to credit approval. Credit or debit balances in a customer's account(s) may be offset by any other outstanding balance owed by or to the customer. Please allow 4 to 6 weeks for delivery. Offer available while quantities last.

**Your Privacy**—The Reader Service is committed to protecting your privacy. Our Privacy Policy is available online at www.ReaderService.com or upon request from the Reader Service.

We make a portion of our mailing list available to reputable third parties that offer products we believe may interest you. If you prefer that we not exchange your name with third parties, or if you wish to clarify or modify your communication preferences, please visit us at www.ReaderService.com/consumerschoice or write to us at Reader Service Preference Service, P.O. Box 9062, Buffalo, NY 14240-9062. Include your complete name and address.

HSE15